A DETECTIVE'S
HEART

A Novel

by

SIOUX DALLAS

CCB Publishing
British Columbia, Canada

A Detective's Heart: A Novel

Copyright ©2012 by Sioux Dallas
ISBN-13   978-1-77143-011-1
First Edition

Library and Archives Canada Cataloguing in Publication
Dallas, Sioux, 1930-
A detective's heart : a novel / written by Sioux Dallas. – 1st ed.
ISBN 978-1-77143-011-1
Also available in electronic format.
Additional cataloguing data available from Library and Archives Canada

Cover images:
1) Female detective: © Can Stock Photo Inc. / piedmont_photo
2) Eyes: courtesy Lumen Design Studio, is in the public domain

Disclaimer: This is a book of pure fiction, a product of the author's imagination, and does not represent any person, living or dead.

Publisher: CCB Publishing
             British Columbia, Canada
             www.ccbpublishing.com

BOOKS WRITTEN BY SIOUX DALLAS

First Experience

Sharon

Desperate Wish

L i i s a

Death in Three Quarter Time

The Perfect Spouse

Montana Madness

Dangerous Hilarity

Amish Dilemma

A Detective's Heart

And coming soon:

Amish Promise: A Sequel to Amish Dilemma

The Snowman Murder

PROLOGUE

Those who hope in the Lord will renew their strength
They will soar on wings like eagles;
they will run and not grow weary
They will walk and not be faint.
Isaiah 40:31

My beloved father, Andrew Jackson Rutherford, was an Auxiliary Policeman for the town of Appalachia, Virginia for several years, as well as a coal mine inspector for safety.

I've always been interested in learning about law enforcement work. In the early 1950s, while teaching school, finishing college, and working with my church obligations, I took eighteen courses to earn a degree as a Private Investigator. My interest has remained keen. In fact, I still have my certificate and my badge. I'm only sorry I'm not presently in any physical condition to pursue an occupation of law enforcement.

This book is written differently than any I've written before. I hope you will accept and enjoy it. At the end of the book, under the pages "Dear Readers", I've included some historical facts about the first female detectives in the early and middle eighteen hundreds.

As usual I've included some recipes of the area about which I'm writing.

So many of you have told me that you look for the

recipes first before you read the book. I hope you enjoy these.

In all my books, I've taken true news and events and spun a story around them. Of course the characters are fictional. I'm still amazed at the number of men who read my books. God bless you all, and thank you sincerely.

CHAPTER ONE

Hannah Rutherford ambled across Oak Street, in Myrtle Beach, South Carolina, looking with pride and a little trepidation at her brand new office:

THE LOST CAUSE DETECTIVE AGENCY
HANNAH RUTHERFORD
INVESTIGATOR

Lost Cause, not because she was lacking, but because she took on cases that offered little or no encouragement to the client. With her reward money for finding the kidnapped child and turning in the offender, her pension from her deceased husband's work, and her inheritance from her maternal grandparents, she felt that she should give back to the community that had been so faithful to her.

Her heart was a little heavy knowing she had set out on a sea that she was not truly prepared for and was sailing on faith and intestinal fortitude, Hannah's father, Andrew Rutherford, was a well-known, successful prosecuting attorney and wanted Hannah to follow in his footsteps. Because she was an only child, he had wrapped his heart and life around her. His wife, Hannah's mother, had been worshipped by him. When she died with cancer soon after Hannah was born, he almost lost his mind. His sister, Marilee, had helped take care of Hannah until she had to retire due to crippling arthritis. Andrew kept Hannah close and made her the heart and center of his life. She tried to follow in his footsteps, but liked law enforcement better, first as a police officer and now as an investigator.

Bouncing gaily into the office she greeted her small staff with sincere love and appreciation. Her golden hair framed a lovely face, not beautiful, but attractive. Eyes as blue as a summer sky sparkled with love of life.

Victoria Stallard, a perky twenty-four year old college graduate was suffering after a drunk driver ran up on the sidewalk and ran over her. She now had braces on one leg and chronic pain in her back and leg. It would have been difficult for her to hold a steady job with anyone who required a nine to five employment or a minimum of forty hour a week. She was grateful for Hannah's understanding and made a promise to herself to love Hannah and be loyal, faithful and helpful. Her ebony face was always smiling and kind.

Hannah, too, had a back injury that left her in almost constant pain.

She had been following a two hundred pound plus carjacker and pedophile. He turned and tackled her landing on her. She had called for back-up and he was arrested but Hannah suffered a painful back.

Herbert Mueller, better known as Herb, was a thirty - two year old ex policeman with two years of law study. He had been a viable officer with a glowing future. He had started studying law with the intention of becoming an attorney. During his second year of study, his wife of eighteen months, hugged him and told him they were expecting their first child. They were both ecstatic and looking forward to the birth.

One day she had gone to the bank to deposit his paycheck. A bank robbery had resulted in her death and the loss of the eight month fetus. Three men, armed, came into the bank and had a shootout with an off duty policeman. She had been hit in the stomach and chest by stray bullets.

Herb had been so crushed he began to drink and didn't report for work or classes. He was given a warning and finally fired from the force. Hannah had offered him a chance to shake loose from the grief and alcohol and become a useful worker again and gain self confidence. Hannah encouraged him to take pride in his work and in his daily life. He would lay down his life for her.

"Good morning all," Hannah burbled with love of life and joy in her choice of future. She stood barely five feet five inches but faced her cases as if she were six feet and two hundred pounds instead of one ten. She had just turned twenty-eight last week.

"Hey boss," Victoria limped over to give Hannah a quick hug. Her own dark eyes were sparkling and full of joy. Her curly dark hair was styled to suit her five feet four frame. Thankfully she weighed only one hundred five pounds or she would suffer trying to carry more weight with her injuries. Her heart-shaped light milk chocolate face was always smiling and pleasant to see. The drunk driver who plowed on to the sidewalk and ran her down did not take away her sweet personality.

Herb lumbered toward the front from a back office. He picked Hannah up and swung her around. His six-three frame was too heavy carrying two hundred eighty pounds, but he was trying to cut out the desserts and tighten his muscles with daily exercise. His green eyes and wavy chestnut hair were ideal for his tanned complexion and dimples.

"Put me down, you oaf," Hannah laughingly ordered.

"Yes, ma'am," he answered with mock bow as he carried her to an office down the hall and deposited her at her desk.

"What has gotten into you?" Hannah asked laughing.

"Look around you," both Herb and Victoria spoke as one.

Taking her first look around didn't satisfy her curiosity until she looked at her newly painted cream walls. Her certificates from college, her law degree, her license to operate and all necessary certificates were framed in beautiful soft pine and hung with care. A large Peace Lily stood in a tub near the floor to ceiling six feet wide window. Light blue vertical blinds covered the window. Beside it was a private door leading to the outside. Two tall metal filling cabinets were in a corner. A new blue carpet, with darker swirls of blue was on the floor showing her polished oak desk and swivel rocker padded oak chair to the best advantage

"When was this done? When I left here Friday this room was empty and smelling of fresh paint."

"We came back on Saturday and did the work so you'd be surprised this morning," Victoria beamed.

"Yeah, my brother-in-law, Merle Boggs, agreed to help. He and my sister are so relieved that I've turned my life round that they're willing to do anything I ask," Herb stated with a grin. "Come see the rest of our space."

Hannah kicked off her spike heels and padded across the hall to the office that Herb used. She was pleased to see a beige runner on the long hall. In the room used by Herb, the walls were the same cream color and his certificates were also framed and on the walls. His oak desk was bigger than Hannah's and the chair was a high-backed, swivel rocker that would accommodate his huge frame. There was a four by six window with blue vertical blinds in his office. Two large filing cabinets were against one wall. A private door was near a corner that would allow him to come and go from the alley without coming through the front.

Next door to Hannah's office was a large conference room with a long table and six comfortable high-backed padded chairs. A table in one corner held materials for coffee, tea, or snacks. A large water cooler burbled in a corner. Two long six by three windows were up high.

Across the hall was a small, well-equipped kitchen with a stove and a microwave, a side by side refrigerator, a sink with a disposal, a table and four chairs. The floor was a mahogany and tan tile. The window was a three by six and high on the outer wall. There was a closet and a counter with several drawers under it. A four slice toaster sat on the counter.

At the end of the hall was a rest room with a sink, a wall dryer, two stalls, a five by three vertical mirror and a comfortable couch.. The two windows were about two by three and high on the outer wall. A small closet held supplies. Mahogany and tan tiles were on this floor.

At the very end was an emergency door with an alarm. Bright motion lights were outside over the door and safety lights on poles over the small parking space for the office. They walked to the front where Victoria reigned behind a large, polished oak desk. On it was a rolodex and a complicated phone system. A computer and a printer were on a table in the corner sitting on an L to her desk. She only had to swing her swivel chair from one to the other. Behind her were four large filing cabinets and a police scanner sitting on top of one of the cabinets. Across from her desk was a water fountain and paper cups in a dispenser beside it. A cream-colored wastebasket sat proudly between the dispenser and a waiting area.

Four comfortable chairs were spaced along the wall with a glass-topped table holding magazines. The walls here were cream and the carpet was the same blue color that was in the private offices. A public restroom was in the corner.

There were two wide front doors that could both be opened to permit a large object to come through. Six by eight tall windows were on either side of the front door. Inside under each window was a shelf built to hold plants or whatever suited the occupants of this office.

By the end of the day two floral shops had sent small plants and potted trees for the front office. Several business people had stopped by to welcome them to the street and to satisfy their own curiosity.

Outside, flanking the front door, were two lovely, large terra-cotta pots. Inside each pot was a Dwarf Alberta spruce, suitable for decorating such as at Christmas. A built-in window box held petunias and snapdragons.

The office was open for business by nine each morning. Hannah usually jogged for three miles starting at six AM and then ran home for a shower and to dress. She ate breakfast when she came to the office. She waved and called a greeting to all she saw on her way to work. Everyone seemed to respect and like the young woman. Everyone that knew her said, "Hannah has a heart of gold and it is as big as all outdoors."

Hannah and her staff were so tickled with the first ad for the business that was in the local paper that Herb also framed that and hung it in the front. Hannah had been very careful to notify the public that she would be willing to listen to any problems without charging a fee and any fee would depend on how much time and work had to be done. Privately she had told Victoria and Herb that they would represent anyone free of charge that was in financial trouble that wasn't their own fault and if they needed help.

The business had only been open for a week, but Hannah was pleased with the response they'd gotten. She felt in her heart that the business would build to fill all of the filling cabinets with documents. A plaque hung on the wall for all to see as soon as they entered the agency. The plaque read:

I can do all things through Christ who strengthens me.

CHAPTER TWO

They had been open two months and had a pleasing amount of clients and work. Victoria was proving to have a keen mind and was learning a lot about laws and court proceedings. She was working toward earning her license to be a detective.

One morning, while on her run, Hannah saw a man sitting on the grass beside City Hall, 937 Broadway, not far from her office. He was dressed as a homeless person might be dressed and hadn't shaved in a long time. As she came near him, he looked straight at her and she was shocked to see intelligent grey eyes. She waved but he quickly ducked his head and looked away.

Her heart went out to him hoping he was going to the shelters and getting food and a bed. He seemed to be in the general vicinity each time she saw him. She never got close enough to see much about him or to talk to him.

She didn't see him for a few days, and, since the weather was getting cooler, she hoped he was inside somewhere. He had previously played a guitar and sang. A few people were dropping coins in a box in front of him.

On a Thursday, in late October, she was late starting her run because a stray dog had shown up at her door and she fed him and made a bed for him in her garage. She had left a bowl of water with the intention of going back during the day to check on him.

She had run an oval through town and about a half mile outside of town through a less than desirable neighborhood. Crossing the street, she started running back. Between the first house in the neighborhood and the main street was an empty lot that was usually full of trash consisting of beer bottles, food containers and other trash. She saw a pile of clothing and thought someone had tossed trash out.

It's time we citizens took the responsibility of cleaning this eye sore up. I'll see what that is and come back later with bags to pick up some of this.

Jogging closer she was shocked to see a person inside the rags. Dropping to her knees beside the person, she felt for a pulse and was relieved to find one, weak, but there. She turned the body slightly and saw that the person was a man who had been beaten and apparently left for dead. Looking more closely she gasped when she recognized the homeless man that she had seen several days before at City Hall. His guitar and coin box were gone.

Pulling her cell phone from a pocket she touched 9-1-1 and waited for help to come. Paramedics and police came. The officer that took the report seemed to be annoyed that she could not give him any information. One of the paramedics was a young woman who told Hannah they would take him to Seacoast Medical Center. Hannah told them she would go home to shower and dress and then be in to sign the papers as person responsible for the bills.

"That's a real nice woman," the paramedic said.

The officer grunted. "She can afford to be. Her grandfather left her a fortune and her husband was killed in an explosion that was caused by the carelessness of his employer. She got a nice sum from his death. She was working in a place that made software computer parts.

"Well, I still say she's a nice woman. I've heard how she gives to the needy and helps the underdog. She could have been selfish and stuck up and kept it all for herself." The young woman jerked her head at the officer as if to say, "so there".

In the excitement Hannah had almost forgotten about the dog. He was obviously glad to see her and wanted to play and be friendly. He seemed to be healthy, but was a little thin as if he had not eaten lately.

She called Jim Martin, a veterinarian friend and told him of the dog. "He's young. I'm guessing him to be a little over a year old. He's a black Labrador and still puppy playful. I'm feeding him and giving him water, but I'd like for you to check if he has a microchip."

'Sure, Hannah. Bring him in. That tears me up. Some people move off and leave an animal behind because they can't have one where they're going. Or sometimes one is stolen and it gets away and wanders in a strange place bewildered and wondering why he isn't loved. I'll look at him for you. Are you going to keep him?"

"No. I wish I could. He's a darling, loving dog, but I'm not always here all day and sometimes I'm gone for several days. It wouldn't be fair to an animal. Could you please help me find a good home for him?"

"I'll try. Have you named him?"

"Oh, no. If I name him, it will be even harder to give him up. I'll see you tomorrow."

She hugged and petted the dog for a minute and then apologized to him.

"I'm sorry little man. I know I just got home, but duty calls and I have to go out again. You've been fed and have water and I've made you a nice soft bed here. I'll even leave a stuffed toy with you. Please don't tear it apart for I've had it for years. Be a good boy."

Hannah hurried into the medical center, her hair still damp from her shower. She had to stop at the main desk and fill out some papers that she would be responsible for the bills for the homeless man. "Have you found out his name?" she asked the nurse.

"No, we haven't, but the sheriff and the chief of police have both been in. It's strange, but they seem to either know him or know something about him."

Hannah thanked her and walked to room 236 on the second floor. The elevator ride up had given her time to think. *Why would the two law men be interested in a homeless man? I'll find out.*

Hannah approached room 236 and saw there was no name in the pocket on the door. She carefully opened the door and slipped into the room. The first thing she noticed was the odor. It smelled like a hospital. *Of course, idiot. What else would it smell like?*

She walked quietly to the bed and looked down at the man who had been hooked up to several machines. The sound of machines working to keep him alive was evident. Hannah wondered how such a young looking man was in this mess. In spite of the injuries from the beating, she could see he was good looking.

He had been shaved and bathed and was now wearing a hospital gown.

He had thick black hair and a surprisingly smooth skin. She jumped in guilt and surprise when his grey eyes opened and he looked at her. She didn't know whether he was cognizant enough to know where he was.

She placed a compassionate hand on his shoulder and spoke to him. "Hello. You don't know me. My name is Hannah Rutherford. I have a detective agency and I've seen you when I was jogging. I know you can't talk now, but I don't want you to worry. I'm paying for your care so you have nothing to worry about except resting and getting better. I won't tire you out now, but I'll be checking in again soon."

He tried to shake his head and made garbled sounds, but no distinguishable words were understandable.

"Please don't make yourself feel worse. I'll be in again soon and later when you're able to talk, we'll have a good visit. I wish you could tell me if you need, or want, anything."

He lifted the hand that had an IV needle stuck in the back of it and made motions with his fingers. Hannah finally realized that he was trying to show her that he could write.

"You've had enough excitement today. It's too soon after your injuries, so I'll leave and let you rest, but I promise to come again soon and I'll bring a pad and pen for you."

She gently patted his shoulder while he closed his eyes in obvious frustration. Hannah quietly left and walked to the nurses' station. A young nurse was looking at information on the computer and writing on patients' files. "Excuse me," Hannah spoke softly. The nurse looked up and smiled.

"Can you tell me anything about the condition of the man in 236? I'm not a relative but I found him and am paying his bills. I'd like to know how badly he's injured and what the doctors are doing to help him."

"You must be Miss Rutherford. We haven't been able to learn his name yet. The sheriff and the chief of police have both been in but they haven't told us anything they've learned about him. As to his condition, I'm not at liberty to give you that information. May I call his doctor to talk to you?"

"Please do. Thank you." Hannah walked over and sat in the cold, green plastic chairs which were far from comfortable.

A few minutes later a man hurried into the room with a white lab coat flapping around his legs. He was wearing a lilac shirt and black trousers under the coat with a grey and black stripped tie hanging loose around his neck.

"Hello. Did you want to see me?"

"Please. I'm Hannah Rutherford. I have the Lost Cause Detective Agency. I found the man in *236* and am paying his bills. Please tell me what you've found about his condition, Dr. ---"

"Sorry about that. You wouldn't believe how rushed I've been. We're short staffed with the flu going around. I'm Dr. Whittaker, Jackson Whittaker. As to my patient, I'm aware that you're paying his bills, however, you are not a relative and I cannot, by law, tell you much. If Sheriff Murphy will give me permission, I'll gladly share."

"All right. I understand. I just wanted to know in case there was anything else I could do for him."

"That's kind of you. I can tell you he has amnesia, apparently due to the blunt force trauma to his head. He has trouble trying to speak, but I'm hopeful that all of his problems will clear soon."

"He signed to show me he wanted to write something for me. I didn't have a pen and paper, but will bring some to him."

"Please don't be in any hurry to bring them. He needs to remain quiet and free of stress for as long as possible."

"Thank you, Doctor. I need to go to work, but I'll be coming by often."

Arriving at home Hannah didn't notice anything wrong at first. She pulled into the double garage careful to not hit the dog. The dog!! Where is he? She ran into the house, not noticing that the door she usually kept locked was open.

"Here, boy. Where are you?"

She heard a weak bark down the hall toward her bedroom. Running in that direction, she began to notice that furniture was turned over, pillows were ripped and obviously someone had been in that didn't belong. She followed the weak moaning sounds to the bathroom and found the dog on his side with what looked like a knife wound.

She quickly knelt beside him and cried, "Oh, I wish you could talk and tell me what happened here. I need to get you to the emergency animal hospital."

Hannah first called 9-1-1 and explained that she had a break and entering and a dog wounded. The police remembered working with her and liked her so they rushed over.

Sgt. Arnold Belcher gave a careful inspection of the entire house along with a rookie, William Brooks, that he was training. William gave a shout of discovery. "Here is a piece of cloth that might have been part of a pant leg, and it has blood on it."

Arnold had an evidence bag and placed the material carefully in the bag. "Good work. Let's hope there's enough here for a DNA. Hannah, have you had threats, or do you have a case involving someone who is angry enough to do this?"

"No to both questions. Forgive me, but I must get this dog to the emergency animal hospital. He apparently did his best to protect my house."

"I didn't know you had a dog. When did you get him?"

"He really isn't mine and it's a long story. I must hurry. Are you going to have an officer stay here until I return, and will you have someone drive by tonight?"

"Sure thing. William and I will stay here and look around more. I want to know how the person got in. Okay, William?"

"Righto Sarg. I'll be glad to stay."

Hannah was grateful when the two men gently placed the dog on a doubled bed sheet and carefully carried him to her car. She had to leave him over night, but was relieved that he would be cared for properly.

In an hour she was back in her home and delighted to find that the two officers had found more clues. The man had broken the glass on the window in a bedroom at the back and side of the house. Apparently he had gone to check the garage for something to steal and the dog had charged him and chased him back through the house. They found a shoe print in the dog's blood and fingerprints on a door frame. He had not had time to do much damage and he had not taken anything of value. But what was he looking for? He had a bite on a leg that would need care, and torn pants.

Hannah thanked the officers after they nailed a piece of plywood over the broken window and called in the report. They asked for a patrolman to drive by every hour or as often as possible. They left when their radio blasted out that there had been a fight and a shooting at a bar downtown.

That night at home Hannah's phone rang four times. When she answered, there was no communication, just breathing. She finally lost patience and yelled out, "Look, if you're too afraid to speak to me, don't bother calling. Come into my office any time and I'll be glad to listen to you."

There was a sound as if someone had taken in a breath and then a raspy voice spoke, "Mind your own business and stay out of that which doesn't concern you. If you want to live or if you want your staff to stay healthy, you'll listen and heed." The phone was gently cut off. She held her phone a few seconds more and then hung up.

The note on her ID screen stated, "unavailable". Star 69 didn't show a number either. She realized the call could have been made from a throw-away phone.

She carefully wrote, Tuesday, October 24, 8:20 pm on a pad near her phone, and the message the caller had left. She had been in the law enforcement business too long to ignore even a crank call. The note would help her remember when she received the puzzling message. What was she involved in that was none of her business? Why would it be important enough for this unsub (unknown subject) to threaten her and her staff?

Should she report it to the sheriff or wait and talk to Victoria and Herb?

Should she mention it to anyone? What did the caller mean? She decided to wait and discuss it with Victoria and Herb.

Hannah was not easily frightened and felt sure she was safe in her own home. In this case, her mistake was in being too sure of herself. She would regret it later.

The next day she had a call from the veterinarian. "Hannah, my sister's eight year old daughter lost her dog this week when he ran into the road and was hit by a car. They've seen this dog you brought in. My niece has already named him, Soldier because he was wounded in battle.. Do you mind if they take him home and love him?"

"Of course not. I can't be at home with an animal and it isn't fair to them. I am so happy that he'll have a good home and will be wanted and loved. Thank you. I'll try to find time to get by and visit them and tell them how grateful I am that they're giving him a good home. He's a loving dog and will be a good companion for your niece. He'll also be very protective."

"Thank you, Hannah. That relieves my mind. I know we spoil my niece, but the dog will have a good home."

CHAPTER THREE

She yawned broadly and deeply as she stretched her body in every direction she could. Keeping her eyes closed against the surprising morning glare, she stretched again. Snapping her eyes open she recoiled when the clock radio blared "Boogie Woogie Bugle Boy". *Eight O'clock! Oh, I've overslept. Radio?! When did I get a radio?*

Sliding a leg from under the covers she was disgusted to discover she was wearing jeans, socks and blouse. Worse yet, the clothes were stiff with blood. Sitting groggily on the side of the bed, and looking at the brownish snake - skin boots she had left at odd places on the floor, she observed that they were also blood stained. One boot was lying over the door sill and the other was under the window at the head of her bed.

Puzzled, she looked around the room. *What happened? Where have I been? Where did this blood come from? Am I in trouble some how? Why can't I remember what happened? Is this my blood?*

The unanswered questions only made her dizzy. Dragging herself to the bathroom she hurriedly dropped her clothes in a heap, and standing in front of a full-length mirror, examined her body. *No wounds. Thank God the blood isn't mine. But whose?* **"Elizabeth Ann Corelli, what in the world have you been up to?"** she asked herself. *Where am I?*

Running the water as hot as she could stand it, she showered and shampooed her hair twice. After drying she slipped into a ankle-length blue silk robe and toe less and back less cotton velour bedroom slippers with a butterfly embroidered on the top of each piece crossing the ball of the foot.

Beth sat on a stool in front of a dresser mirror while using a blow dryer to style her natural curly strawberry - blond hair. It was finally growing out from a bad cut and was now collar length. She wanted it to the top of her shoulder blades. Worried hazel - green eyes looked through long lashes. A smooth, healthy complexion required no cosmetics although a little coral lipstick and a light beige powder were often applied.

Sighing deeply she looked at the completed project and decided it didn't look too bad. She had never been considered a beauty, but her mouth with a bow in it was always smiling and making people feel good around her. Her chin was a little too pointed on her triangular- shaped face giving her a determined look. An interesting and -- yes-- attractive face. People had always said, "Beth has a charismatic personality."

A rumbling in her stomach made her aware that she was hungry. *Do I eat here or out?* She looked around the room not truly recognizing the items in it. Making her way past the guest bedroom she came to a small room on the right better known as a den rather than a living room.

On the left, across from the den, was a small room with a floor to ceiling window. On the right, in front of the window was a drop-leaf table that could be opened to seat six. On the wall, across from the table, was a beautiful oak china cabinet filled with expensive looking dishes.

Straight through was a kitchen. On her left was a stove. Beside it was a side by side refrigerator and by the refrigerator was a small room holding broom, cleaning supplies and a vacuum cleaner. On the right, under a window, was a deep, double sink and cabinets overhead. A dishwasher took the space beside the sink.

Timidly she opened the refrigerator door and found a pitcher of orange juice, eggs, butter, jams, raw carrots, raw cauliflower, a bowl of fresh cut fruit and a loaf of bread. There was a jar of instant coffee and some cans of Diet Coke. Not sure how her stomach would receive much food, Beth decided to just have juice and toast. A four slot toaster sat on one side of the stove. *Why does none of this seem familiar to me?*

Seated at the table with two pieces of toast, butter, blackberry jam and a can of Coke, she looked out of the window at an unfamiliar scene. Jumping nearly out of the chair she stood up when the ringing phone hanging on the wall between the dining room and the kitchen blared out.

"Hello." She spoke low.

"Beth? Is that you? Beth? **Beth?** "The person yelled anxiously.

"Yes."

"Beth. It's Connie. Can you hear me? How are you feeling?"

"Do I know you?"

"Beth! Of course you know me. We're best friends and work together. In fact, you're in my apartment."

"Oh. That explains why everything is so strange to me. How did I get here in your apartment?" She was afraid to ask about the blood on her clothes.

"You don't remember? Oh, I bet you have amnesia."

"Whatever. I guess I do. Why am I here and why can't I remember anything except my name?"

"You don't remember the party last night?"

"Party?"

"We gave a going away party for Crystal. Remember? She's getting married and is leaving to move to Arizona where her husband is working."

"No. I don't remember. How do I know you and Crystal?"

"We work here in the court house in a group of legal secretaries."

"We do?"

"Sure. You don't remember the party. Do you remember slapping Malcolm when he whispered something to you? Then you jumped up and ran out and he was right on your heels."

"Nothing. Why am I here? Where did the blood on my clothes come from? Who is this Malcolm?"

"I had to speak to someone but came after you as quickly as I could. I found you wandering in the parking lot of the Full and Plenty Restaurant. You were covered in blood and couldn't talk. I didn't know what had happened or how you got the blood on you. I just put you in my car and brought you home. You were so out of it, and fought me, that I just managed to take off your boots and put you in my bed. I slept on the couch. I called to ask you if you remembered how you got the blood on you."

"No," she sobbed. "I don't remember."

"Well then. Maybe this news will jog your memory. Let me read it to you. I'll only read the important parts. It seems that after you and Malcolm Baker ran out last night, someone beat him to death. There was so much blood around that it is described as a blood bath. Apparently you were near, or maybe you held him. The police are looking for anyone who has any information on him. I know you would never have killed him. You're too small to have caused that much damage to a man much bigger than you. It just isn't your nature to get so angry anyway. Maybe you saw it happen."

"Now I remember," Beth screamed. There was a small clunk and a loud plop. Silence.

"Beth? Beth? Are you still there? Are you okay? I'm coming home."

CHAPTER FOUR

Connie Ackerman ran into her apartment with Ben Goodman hot on her heels. They found Beth lying unconscious on the floor with the phone buzzing as it hung, down the wall, off the hook.

"Beth. Wake up." Ben gently slapped her face while Connie wet a white tea towel to rub Beth's face and wrists.

"Is she all right, Ben?"

"I don't know yet. You said she had amnesia and now she has lost consciousness. What caused her to have amnesia?"

"I'm not sure. When she rouses, maybe she'll be able to tell us." Connie didn't want to tell how she found Beth until she knew more about the entire situation. Ben was a friend, a new attorney, but the less people know about Beth, the less she would have to explain.

"Connie, call 9-1-1. With amnesia Beth may have something very serious and we're not medical people. We can't help her. Does she have health insurance?"

"Yes, the same that all of us have who work at the courthouse."

"Then please make the call."

Connie made the call and then placed a rolled-up towel under Beth's head. *I'm glad Beth had a chance to clean up before she had to be taken to the hospital. I need to find her bloody clothes and put them away until I get a chance to ask for advice on how to help her handle this.*

"Excuse me a moment, Ben. I'm going to run back to the bedroom and get her handbag. She'll need her medical cards and maybe her driver's license."

Connie ran back and found the shoulder bag where she had left it on a chair. She hurriedly picked up the bloody clothes and placed them in a laundry bag from the bathroom. She stuffed the bag into the towel closet in the bathroom and hoped she would not get into trouble because of this.

Ben had opened the door for the paramedics as Connie came back into the kitchen. "May I ride in the ambulance with you? Beth has been very sick and will feel more secure if she sees me when she wakes up."

The two men looked at each other with raised eyebrows. "I guess it's okay," one answered. Jeff will be in the back with you. I'm Alan and I'll be driving."

Connie turned to Ben. "Ben, do you mind following and bringing my car? I'm sure I'll need it later."

"No need to ask. I'll be happy to do what I can."

"Oh, and Ben, maybe you can ask Jerry to help you. I left Beth's car in the restaurant parking lot last night. There will be too many questions from the wrong people if it's left there long."

"I'll take care of it. Don't worry about a thing except helping Beth."

Thank God I'm the only one who knows about the bloody clothes, Connie thought as she climbed into the back of the ambulance and took Beth's hand.

Dr. August West came into the waiting room to find Connie slumped in a despondent pose. "Miss Ackerman?"

"Yes." Connie jumped up at full attention. "How is Beth?"

"Miss Corelli is doing well physically. As you said she does have amnesia. I will call it selective amnesia meaning. She has had a traumatic event and has elected to put it out of her mind sometimes these last a few hours, or even days. In rare instances they may last for weeks. Miss Corelli seems to be in excellent physical condition so I'm going out on a limb and guess that it will not be more than a few days before she decides to join us. Then we shall find out what caused her to shut out the rest of the world."

He smiled. "Do you have any questions? Since you are not a relative, I can't give you any more information than that."

"Beth is like a sister to me. We have been friends for years; went to school together, work together and socialize together. I need to know all you can tell me. I'll be with her when she recovers and I will need to be the best help she needs. She has no relatives here."

"I appreciate that, but policy is policy," he chuckled. "I don't always agree, but my hands are tied. Now if you'll excuse me, I have other patients."

"May I see Beth?"

"If it will make you feel better. She won't even know you're with her because we're keeping her under light sedation. I'll tell the nurses to allow you to sit with her as long as you don't disturb her."

"Oh, I'll follow orders. I want to be with her. I'll sit quietly and read. Tomorrow I'll being needlework and do something with it. Thank you, Doctor."

Another day passed slowly as Connie agonized beside Beth. She hardly left her side to shower and change clothes. Ben came each day and was worried about Connie.

"Connie, they're taking good care of Beth. You need to take better care of yourself. If you get run down and collapse, you'll be in here and you sure won't be any help to Beth."

"You're sweet, Ben, to be concerned. I appreciate it, but everyone must understand I'm not leaving her until she recovers completely." She didn't dare tell them that she was afraid for Beth that she might say something either while she was out or if she woke up and didn't know what had happened.

The third day Beth's eyes fluttered; she moaned and became restless.

Connie called a nurse to check her.

"She's fine, Miss Ackerman. She's just waking up. It's possible this will all be over in a few hours." The nurse left and Connie took Beth's hand.

"Beth. Beth, can you hear me? It's time to wake up. Please open your eyes and look at me. Come one, Beth. You can do it."

Another soft sigh and Beth opened her eyes. She looked around puzzled and focused on Connie.

"Oh, hi there, Connie. Where am I?"

"You're in Seacoast Medical facility and have been in here for a few days."

"Really! Why am I here? I don't feel sick."

"You're not really sick. You've had amnesia and would not wake up. Lazy girl. You've been sleeping almost three days."

Beth sat up. "I have?! What happened?"

"You tell me, girlfriend. First, you know who I am."

"Of course, silly."

"Do you remember the party we attended to wish Crystal a fond farewell as she went west to be married?'

"Yes. I'm glad it was such a great party. She had a lot of useful, lovely gifts and what a money tree." Judge Ronald Kress had brought in a small limb with a few tiny branches. He had placed a hundred dollar bill on one branch and ask everyone present to place whatever they could afford to make a money tree for the couple. So many people had placed tens, twenties and loads of ones until the tree was completely full. When counted, there was over five hundred dollars.

Connie quickly, whispering, told Beth of the death of Malcolm and how Beth had first had amnesia and then became unconscious. Beth nodded sadly.

"Now I remember. I heard Malcolm calling to me, but I hurried to my car. I was in such a hurry to get away that I dropped my keys in the floor. It was too dark to see, so I had to lean over and hunt for them. When I sat up I heard a commotion. There were three men beating Malcolm. Blood was flying all over the place. I was afraid to let them know I was there so I laid over in the seat and was quiet until I couldn't hear any more noises. I slowly sat up and got out of the car. Malcolm was on the ground and I ran to him to see if

I could help him. I guess I realized he was dead. The last I remember, I held him against my chest and cried."

"Oh, Beth. I found you wandering around in a fog; not talking or knowing what was going on. I took you to my apartment and kept you until I decided you needed medical help that I couldn't give." Silence.

"Beth, you are innocent of Malcolm's death. However, if word gets out that you saw the men, the criminals might be afraid you can identify them and will try to kill you."

"Connie, what am I going to do? I must tell the police what I saw. Will they blame me or arrest me?"

"I don't see how they can do either, but you need legal advice."

"I don't want an attorney. I can't imagine why I would need one."

Connie sat up straight. "I have an answer. I don't know the woman personally, but I've heard great things about her. A woman, Hannah Rutherford, was a policewoman and then felt she wanted more action. She has opened her own investigative agency. We can ask her for advice at least. She can tell us in what direction to go from here."

"That sounds good. Do you know how to contact her?"

"I can find out. Do you want me to make the first contact? If she is interested, she can see you then." She was pleased that Beth agreed.

CHAPTER FIVE

The next day Connie walked into The Lost Cause Detective Agency. She was met by Victoria.

"Good morning! Welcome to The Lost Cause Detective Agency. My name is Victoria. How can I help you?"

"I need to see Miss Rutherford."

"Do you have an appointment or do you want to make one?"

"Neither. This is vitally important. A young woman's life is at stake. I need to see Miss Rutherford as soon as possible. Right now, please."

Herb heard the excited voice and came out to see if Victoria need a backup. "Good morning. Is Victoria helping you?"

"She's very kind, but it's vitally important that I see Miss Rutherford **now**."

"I'm sorry. She's out on a case now, but should be back around one if you can wait that long."

"I guess I have no choice. Please make sure that I get to see her. I shall return. I'm going down to that diner I saw to get some lunch. I'll be back. Thank you both."

"Miss," Victoria called after her. "May I have your name?"

"I'm sorry. I'm so disturbed that I have been very rude. Forgive me. My name is Connie Ackerman."

On the dot of one Connie was in the agency ready to talk to Hannah. At one twenty Hannah walked in looking weary and rumpled. She nodded politely at Connie who jumped up and said, "Miss Rutherford? I must speak to you. It's vitally important to the life of an innocent young woman."

"Hannah, this is Connie Ackerman. She came in earlier to see you."

"Please come back to my office. I need to kick off these shoes and sit in a comfortable chair." Connie eagerly trailed after her.

Hannah did kick off her shoes, got a glass of ice and a Diet Coke and offered to share something with Connie.

"No, thank you. I just need your advice. I'm willing to pay you. I'm not here expecting free service."

Hannah chuckled. "It wouldn't be the first time I dispensed free service. Now tell me what you're so concerned about."

Connie carefully and concisely told Hannah the entire story.

Hannah listened politely. The more she heard the more her heart ached for Beth.

"There's no need to tell you that it's always best to face any situation at the first and tell the truth. Beth could have had an attorney present to advise her and protect her interests. The only trouble I see at the moment is the danger to Beth if the men who killed Malcolm hear of this and are afraid she might identify them. Of course she might be charged with obstructing justice. I'll talk to Beth and get her statement first hand and maybe she'll be able to tell me a bit more. In the meantime both of you keep quiet until I get a chance to talk to Beth. Bring the bloody clothes to me and remember -say nothing to anyone."

Connie left feeling a little better that someone in authority was looking into the situation and would advise her and Beth without telling on them.

I'm not sure *what we're doing is lawful but I need to trust Miss Rutherford and allow her time to investigate and advise us as to the best possible action.*

Connie breathed easier and was more at peace now that she had shared Beth's calamity with a qualified person. She was glad she had kept the bloody clothes and had not mentioned Beth's involvement to anyone.

"You mean she wants to talk to me?' Beth stated with a trembling voice. "Won't she go to the police and report me?"

"No, silly. She is working for you and we must trust her. Now when can you meet her?"

"Name the date and time and I'll certainly be there."

"Great! I'll call her now and make an appointment." Connie went in the next room of her apartment to make the call. Beth sat nervously not sure that she was doing the right thing. *Connie is a dear, trusted friend. I'll appreciate anything that she and this woman can do for me. How I wish I had never seen the beating and murder. But I did and I must face reality.*

Connie came back with a big smile. "Miss Rutherford will see us at nine tomorrow morning. Now you get a good night's sleep and I'll fix a good breakfast for you before we leave. We'll go together. Place yourself in God' hands for you have done nothing wrong. Go to bed and rest."

Beth was so nervous that she would not have gone if Connie had not insisted. She was put somewhat at ease by

Victoria's warm welcome. Meeting Hannah was not as scary as she imagined.

Connie recognized Beth's nervousness and opened the conversation by reminding Hannah how she had found Beth wandering and took her to her own apartment. "I must tell you, we have not spoken of this to another soul. We are the only two who know absolutely what Beth experienced. A young attorney did come to her aid when she fainted, but he doesn't know why or what had transpired."

Hannah was very business-like and friendly so that Beth became very much at ease. She told Hannah how Malcolm was a bore and had whispered unwelcome comments to her. She then told of leaving, dropping her keys and looking up to see the beating which she learned later was a murder.

Hannah looked thoughtful. "I can understand your trepidation. It isn't apparent whether the suspects knew they were being observed?"

"Not to my knowledge. It all happened so quickly. They were outside a building where anyone could step out at any moment and discover them."

"Umm. I'm sure they left in a hurry. They probably did not look around and have no idea that they were seen. Could you identify them or recognize them if you saw them again?"

"I don't think so. They were constantly moving and I was in shock."

"I shouldn't say this, but if you tell this to the police, someone might let it slip that you were there. The suspects don't know that you can't identify them and they would certainly come after you. I'm going to stick my neck out and say let's just keep this with us three for the time being. I'll go to the police station and ask to see the report and find out how far their investigation has gone. Is that all right with you?"

Beth looked at Connie and raised her eyebrows. Connie nodded. "We came to you for advice and guidance. We would be stupid if we didn't cooperate with you. What happens next?"

"Be patient. I'll contract you as soon as I find something to share."

"Great," Connie was relieved as was Beth. "How much do we owe you?"

"Let's leave the talk of payment until I have something to tell you and know how much I'm going to have to be involved. Remember just us three."

Beth popped up feeling much at ease. "Thank you so much."

"Don't thank me yet. We haven't gotten anywhere yet."

"I thank you for allowing me to tell you my story and for giving me the comfort of knowing you're on the job."

They left and Hannah wrote some notes and placed them in a locked filing cabinet. She then went out to the front.

"Victoria, I'm going to run by Seacoast and check on the man with amnesia that I found. After that I'm going by the police station and read some reports. I'll have my cell phone in case you need me in an emergency. I'll come by here late to check on mail and any phone calls I need to answer. Herb is out on a case, so keep the phone handy in case you need help. Check all locks on doors and windows before you leave if you're gone before I get back."

"Good deal, Boss." She saluted. "I'm yo lil ole man."

"Silly. Are you trying to pretend to talk Southern? You failed."

Hannah laughed and walked out.

At Seacoast Hannah was greeted by several nurses. She had been checking on the man and they were aware that she was paying the bills. She spoke briefly to the two at the nurses' station and started walking back to Room 236.

"Miss Rutherford," one nurse called, "the man has gone."

Hannah whirled around. "Gone!?" She came back to the station. "Where did he go? Did he regain his memory?"

The nurses looked at each other. "We don't know any more than what is written on the medical report. All we know is that Chief Ed Wingate personally came and got him. He took him somewhere and said he would be responsible for him."

"Well, was the man talking and did he tell anything about himself or what happened to him?"

The nurses looked at each other. One spoke. "As I said, we don't know any more than is written on the medical records. There is no record of him telling anything or what his name is."

"Why would the Chief take him and be responsible?" Hannah asked bewildered.

"You know as much as we do. Sorry. We can't tell you any more."

"Okay. Thank you ladies. Do you know where the Chief took him?"

"No."

"Sorry to bother you." She turned to walk off.

"No bother. I just wish we could help you. Truthfully, we'd like to know."

Hannah smiled at them and left. *Why is the Chief interested? Where could he take him? Is the Sheriff in on this? There is only one way to find out.*

Hannah decided the walk would be good for her. She appreciated the time to think as she walked to the police station. It was apparently a shift change because uniformed and plain clothes officers were milling around with some shaking hands and either saying hello or so long.

"Excuse me, please." Hannah tried to pass by a small knot of men and women.

"Hannah? Hannah Rutherford, is that you?" The call came from an older woman at the front desk. "My goodness, child. I've heard some nice things about you, but I've missed seeing your sweet smile. Come give me a hug."

Hannah smiled broadly and made her way to the desk through a group that insisted on hugging her or slapping her on the back as she walked across the room. She was appreciative of the fact that she had a good reputation and was well liked. She had worked previously with many of these officers.

The sweet lady, Anna May Harkins, was ready to retire after twenty-six years as a receptionist for the police department. She had been like a mother to Hannah when she first came in as a rookie officer.

Darlene Harwood could not leave her job as dispatcher, but blew a kiss to Hannah and motioned for her to come talk inside the bullet-proof cubicle. She pushed a button to open the door so that Hannah could walk in. Hannah didn't want to take Darlene's attention from her job as she might be needed any second. She just darted in, gave Darlene a hug and a quick word and left.

Just as she stepped out of the booth, Chief Wingate stuck his head out of his office door and called. "Hannah! I heard you were here. Come in and talk a minute. I don't have much time, but I want to see you." He stepped back so that she could walk by him and enter his office. He offered her a chair and then went to sit behind his desk.

"I'm glad to see you, Chief. In fact, I came especially hoping to talk to you."

"It's always a pleasure to see you, Hannah. What can I do for you?"

"I went to see about the man who has amnesia. I have been paying his bills, and was told that you had moved him. I'm interested as a caring person should be about another. Did he regain his memory? Where did you take him?"

"Hannah, Hannah. I do admire your ability to care for the underdog and I know you did a great service for that man. You'll just have to take my word for it. He is part of an ongoing investigation and I can't tell you any of the details. He is in a safe, secluded place and will receive the very best medical care."

"Chief! I worked with you for a long time and you know I can be trusted."

"Yes, I know all of that, but it remains a police investigation. Not many of our present officers know what is going on. I do trust you, but you're no longer one of us."

"Oh, Chief. You don't know how much that hurts."

"I know, my dear, but rules are rules, and, as I remember, you were always a stickler for playing by the book".

"I still am, but I can't help but feel I can help".

"You might do that, but I can't chance getting into hot water for confiding to an - umm - outsider".

"Oh, come on now. How dare you call me an outsider."

"Hannah, I'm going to stick my neck out and share some vitally, important happenings with you. I hope I can count on you to keep it to yourself. Don't even tell your staff until the case is solved."

"Do I have to place my hand on a Bible and swear?"

"No, nothing like that. I do trust you. I've known you most of your life and know and admire your father."

"Thank you, Chief. Now what is it?"

He took a deep breath and picked up a folder. He took some pictures out and handed them across the desk to her. She gasped, but quietly looked through them. "What's the meaning of this?"

CHAPTER SIX

"In the last week, we've found these three bodies down near the waterfront. They have been cut up. They had organs removed from their bodies. Liver, kidneys, and in one case, a heart. I'm afraid some of this so called surgery was begun while the person was still alive."

"Why? Why were the organs removed?"

"Body parts sell for a lot of money. I hope to catch these butchers and catch the medical staff that's buying them."

"It has to be someone with medical knowledge to do this job. Could it be a doctor? Maybe an intern? They don't make enough to pay off their schooling. I can imagine some of them would attempt anything."

"I'm afraid you're right. These cuts were made with a very sharp instrument, possibly a scalpel."

"That's illegal."

"Of course. That's why they operate in secret taking organs and leaving a body. Apparently they are afraid of being caught in the act or they would not leave the bodies where they can easily be found."

"But you don't want me involved."

"That's right. It could be very dangerous."

"You forget all the training I had as a police officer and the experience I've had. I feel qualified."

"I don't doubt that you are, but, I repeat, you're not one of us any more, and I would be heartbroken if something happened to you."

"I do appreciate that, Chief, but ---"

"No buts. Just keep your eyes open. You can tell your staff that you've heard news about this. Just don't tell anyone where you heard it. And don't tell that you've seen the pictures. Remember, we don't know who the unsubs are and I would be devastated if you were overheard, or found, by the wrong person. Your life could be in danger."

"I promise, Chief, and I will stay alert."

He stood and came around to hug her.

"You have a beautiful office, Chief. I don't remember one wall being wonderful-smelling cedar."

"Yes, I had that put in about a year ago."

Hannah looked at the beautiful oak desk and soft leather swivel rocker.

On the desk was a family picture, the Chief, his wife and three children. On the cedar wall were certificates and pictures of him shaking hands with important people. Hannah was proud to know him and knew he was one of the best Chief of Police they ever had.

"Thank you for seeing me, and thank you for the confidence."

"Please don't make me regret it," he begged.

"I shall not. So long. I don't like saying good bye, it's too permanent sounding. I expect to see you again. Oh, I would appreciate reading a police record of the death of Malcolm Baker."

"Sure, but why would you need to see a closed case?"

"Closed? I heard nothing about it."

"That's because we kept it quiet since the mob was involved."

She quickly read the report and was too excited to do anything but hug the Chief and tell him he was a jewel.

They laughed and he walked Hannah out and back to the front. She told everyone there so long and walked out. She hurried back to the office with thoughts running so rapidly through her brain that she didn't notice the black Lincoln that seemed to be following her. She quickly opened the door and almost ran inside.

"Hey gang. Everyone into my office. I have some shattering news."

"I'm right in the middle of a report. Can it wait?" Victory answered.

"Not this time."

Herb lumbered in from his office as Victoria limped into Hannah's office ahead of him.

"Okay, boss. We're here. What has you with such a tight girdle?"

"In the first place, don't call me boss and I DON'T wear girdles, so I don't want to hear that again." She frowned at Herb.

"Uh oh. She's got her knickers in a knot." Herb pretended to whisper while Victoria glared at him and sat down quietly. Herb sat and waited.

"I just heard some disturbing news. I'm not at liberty to tell much about it except to ask you to stay alert. We have a gruesome, unusual crime going on here in our fair city and there's no solution in sight at this moment,"

"Gracious. Are you going to share with us or just sit there looking smug?" Victoria said, squirming in her chair. Her back and leg were aching.

"Patience my child. I have had a shock. I learned today that we have a horrendous crime going on right under our noses. It seems that some ghouls are killing innocent people and cutting out their body parts to sell illegally."

There was a stunned silence and Victoria finally said, almost in a whisper, "I've never heard of such a thing."

Herb gritted his teeth. "How does this affect us? Are we going to work a case concerning this -------?"

"No. We must not get involved in an ongoing investigation unless we are requested to do so. I just want you to be aware of it and keep alert for any signs of this offense. If you are suspicious of someone, or a happening, come talk to me and we'll decide if we need to report to the local police. I assume that, by now, the FBI has been called in. Please, please keep yourselves safe. Victoria, **do not** go out at night alone, and Herb, don't play King Arthur or James Bond. I don't want to lose either one of you."

"I certainly won't go out alone and I sure won't go near the waterfront unless we will be working in that area." Victoria stated nervously.

"You, my dear, won't be working anything except here in the office keeping records and answering the phone. I treasure you, but you are far from being ready to investigate anything."

"Well, I have three cases I'm working now and that's enough. Will there be anything else?" Herb asked rising.

"No. I just want to say I'm so pleased with both of you. I couldn't have chosen better workers or friends. Go. Have a good day. Herb, you look as if you're losing weight. How are you doing?"

"Fine. I have lost ten pounds and I'm working out at the gym whenever I can. I intend to keep with this program until I'm down to about two ten."

"Good for you. I'm proud of you. Please eat properly. You need the right kinds of food for energy and to keep your body healthy."

"I know and I'm serious about it now."

Herb rushed out to his office to finish some notes. Victoria, limping slowly, went back to her desk looking thoughtful. Hannah sighed and swiveled to look out her window at nothing while she thought about her morning. *Where is the man that had amnesia? Why is the Chief keeping him in hiding?* Too many thoughts were rushing through her head. She shook her head and turned to pick up her phone.

"Beth? This is Hannah Rutherford. If you want to come in this afternoon I have some news for you." She listened a moment. "Yes, of course you can bring Connie with you. I shall be glad to see you both. Take care and rest easy. See you around three."

Smiling she turned to her computer to enter some notes on a case and review what she knew of Beth's case.

CHAPTER SEVEN

He lay on his back on the bed looking up at the circling fan. Suddenly he felt as if he was being skinned from the inside out. His stomach felt as if he had swallowed a hand full of broken glass. He twisted and cried in agony.

Blood began to flow from his mouth, nose and eyes. He could hardly breathe. He lay in horror, so much in pain that he could hear his own heart laboring and pounding in his body. No. It was someone pounding on his bedroom door. He sat up in bed grateful to be able to breathe in spite of the fact that he was soaked with perspiration.

What a horrible dream. But was it a dream or a premonition? *I think I know now who is going to kill me and what method he'll try to use.*

"Mr. Harmon! Mr. Harmon! Are you all right? Have you had another nightmare? Lord, help us. You sound like you're dying."

"Thank you Mrs. Morton. Yes, it was another bad dream. I'm fine. How are the children?"

"They're fine, Mr. Harmon. Thank God they didn't hear you. They're still asleep. Do you need anything?"

"No. Thank you, Mrs. Morton. Go back to bed. I hope you can rest. I might get up for a few minutes."

"All right. If you're sure you don't need me. Try to get some rest."

Brian Harmon slowly crawled away from the soaked linens and stood up still feeling off balance. He got clean pajama bottoms out of a dresser drawer and went into his bathroom for a hot shower. His mind was flying around with sad, fearful and angry thoughts.

Two years ago he had kissed his pregnant wife and tiny son and left to fly from New York to Denver, Colorado for a book signing. On the plane he sat by a man who proved to be far too friendly and who insisted on talking most of the way.

"Hello, I'm Thomas Chandler. I'm going to Denver on a business trip. Why are you going?"

Brian hesitated and finally told about his book signing in a huge book store. Tom, as he wanted to be called, was impressed and continued to ask questions and give his unwanted opinions. Finally he turned to Brian and asked, "Are you married?"

"Oh, yes, and I couldn't be happier."

"Are you just saying that because I'm a stranger or do you mean it?"

"I have the best wife any man could ever hope to have. We have a one and a half year old son and she's now pregnant. Yes, I'm happy and satisfied. I hate to be away from her for even a few days."

"Well, Brian. I'm not happy. I was hoping to make a deal with you. I like you and think we could help each other."

"What are you talking about?"

"I was hoping to meet someone with whom I could trade. I think you would keep your mouth shut."

By now Brian was uneasy. The expression in Tom's eyes was strange. "I'm not following you." Brian said uneasily.

"No. I guess you aren't. Forget it."

They were a little over an hour out of Denver when Tom brought up the subject again. "I need someone to kill my wife. Her father is nauseatingly rich and thinks he has me under his thumb. She only wants me so she can pretend to be happily married. I know for a fact that she is having affairs and her old man thinks their family is made of gold. I tried to talk to him about it and he asked me if I enjoyed my life. It was a threat. He doesn't care what his daughter is doing and was, in a way, threatening me to not upset her apple cart."

"Oh. I'm sorry to hear that." By now Brian was wishing he could move.

"I wanted to offer to exchange with you."

"Exchange? Exchange what?"

"Killing our wives."

"What!" Brian spoke louder than he intended and caused several people to turn and look at him. He lowered his voice.

"Are you crazy man? I've never killed anyone or anything in my life and I don't intend to start now. If anyone thinks they're going to harm my wife, I might be tempted to kill them first. You'd better not hurt her or my child - er children."

"Don't get so excited. I was just teasing. I don't love my wife any more, but I don't want her hurt in any way."

"Drop the subject," Brian demanded, "it makes me nervous even thinking about it."

"Sure". Tom snickered, "I just wanted to see how an author's brain would work."

"Explain," Brian said stiffly.

"Let's pretend you're writing a book about two people exchanging plans to kill each other's spouse. How would you go about it?"

"I don't even want to pretend. I don't want to discuss it at all."

"Oh, come on, Brian. Be a sport. It'll help us pass the time. Put your thinking cap on. You might think about it. After all, it would make a good mystery. Now how would you go about it? Pretend we are the two men."

Brian shook his head but began to think it might make a good plot for a book. "Okay," he said reluctantly.

Brian took a shower and dressed to go out. Although the sun was out, the November air was cool and brisk. Mrs. Morton had bathed, fed and dressed Matthew, who was almost three and little Reinata, who was one. Their mother, Eileen, whom Brian had loved with his whole heart, had been killed in a strange one-car accident when Reinata was three weeks old. Brian had hired Mrs. Morton to help him with the children while he worked.

I was always suspicious of Eileen's death. She was an excellent driver and the road wasn't even slick. My nightmare last night clinched it for me. I've been having too many of them. I need to talk to someone about this, but the police will just pass it off as a broken heart, even with my evidence. I'll always love her and I adore my children. They're part of her.

Brian was driving slowly down Oak Street, when a sign caught his eye.

"The Lost Cause Detective Agency! That's what I need." He hurriedly found a parking spot and walked quickly back to the agency.

CHAPTER EIGHT

Herb awakened early one morning and decided to go on to the office and get some paper work finished without interruptions. He unlocked the door and entered his office. Before he sat down he had an urge to get coffee and a doughnut. *No, stupid. You can't lose weight and tone up by eating sweets.* He walked out and jogged down three doors to a diner, buying a large styrofoam cup of coffee with just a small amount of fat free cream.

Hurrying back to the office he was ashamed of himself for leaving the door open. *Wait. I left it unlocked but not open. Oh, good grief. I'm glad we don't carry money in here, but what could someone want? Records! Information!! That's all confidential.* He burst through the front door with a scowl on his face.

A man was walking back and forth obviously agitated.

"OH, I'm so glad to see you. My name is Brian Harmon and my life and my babies' lives are in danger. I need your help desperately."

Brian was five-ten and weighed in at one seventy. He worked out several days a week at the gym, but the back of his neck felt strained looking up at Herb. He decided he felt comfortable with him because the expression on Herb's face was filled with caring and compassion.

"Sure. I'm Herb. Come on back to my office and we'll take care of your business."

Herb smiled and turned to walk back to his office. He had lost another fifteen pounds and was feeling great. He liked Brian at first glance and could see Brian was troubled.

Herb stepped back to allow Brian to enter his office. "Have a seat, Brian. Would you like something to drink -- coffee, soda, water? Or would you like a pastry -- or both?" Herb laughed. "If you could have seen me six weeks ago, you'd have thought I eat everything in here. The truth is I'm very proud of the fact that I've cut back on the calories and am working out on a regular basis. I've lost thirty-five pounds in all."

Brian ran nervous fingers through his light brown hair. His gray eyes were taking in everything in a fearful, sad manner. He tried to smile at Herb. "Congratulations. I work out regularly, also. I sit too much and I enjoy the exercise."

"Great. Now, how can I help you?"

Brian hesitated and took a long breath. "It's a long story and I imagine you will find it unbelievable." Herb sat quietly looking interested. He told Herb about the encounter on the plane and the conversation. "With God as my witness, I loved my wife dearly and it almost killed me to lose her. If I had not had the children, I'd been tempted to do away with myself. My grief was so great I could hardly think, but the children needed me."

Herb nodded. "I can understand that. So you think this Tom character is responsible for the death of your wife."

"I know it" Brian pulled a small rectangular box from his pocket. "Last week Mrs. Morton had the day off. I answered the door and found this hanging in a brown envelope on the outside door handle. Again if I had not had the children, I would have done something drastic. I was frightened and then so angry I could hardly contain myself. My first thought was to hunt him down and kill him. I need to let you listen to this," he said as he took out a small tape player and took a tape from the box. "First, listen and then

I'll explain." He played the tape.

"Okay Brian, you're the brain. How are we going to do this. If we kill each other's wife, we will never be suspected since we aren't friends and don't even live in the same town. You have some great ideas which also make you a successful author." The tape went on to explain the plan.

Brian was now wiping tears from his eyes. "I didn't realize he was taping our conversation and now I know he doctored the tape to make it sound as if all this was my idea. The police are going to think I made arrangements for my darling wife to be murdered. Yesterday I had a phone call which, he told me, could not be traced. He reminded me that he had done as he promised and now it was time for me to kill his wife. He said if I did not, or if I told anyone about this, he would make sure the police thought I was to blame for everything. What am I going to do?" Brian broke down sobbing. "My precious children need me. I've had to be both mother and father to them and I love them more than I can express. Too, I refuse to kill anyone except to protect my family."

Herb was shaken at the audacity of the Tom character. He knew from his experience as a police officer, and his training to become an attorney, that circumstantial evidence can be dangerous at times. He also knew that, with modern technology, a lot could be done to prove the tape had been altered.

"Brian, how long has Mrs. Morton been working for you?"

"Eleven months. Just since Eileen died."

"She can't testify about your relationship with you wife then."

"Yes, she can. We've known her from church since we were married. Our pastor has known us long before we were married and the majority of the church membership can testify for me, and I'm sure they'd all be willing to do so."

"Brian, I'm going to do something I never do. I'm going to suggest that we include your pastor in this discussion."

"Why?" Brian yelped, jumping up.

"Because if Thomas implements a nasty action before we proceed, your pastor will know the truth and can vouch for you."

"I didn't think of that. Should I have gone to him first?"

"No. You have done the right thing. I will say that when I was on the police force I experienced some circumstantial evidence putting people in prison that I wasn't too sure of. I hated it, but I couldn't fight the system."

There was a pause. "I don't know, Herb. I don't feel comfortable letting my pastor know about this. Truthfully? Even though I haven't committed a crime, I still feel dirty."

"Okay, Brian. I respect your feelings. Why don't we wait until I can discuss this with my partner and get back to you?"

He could see how emotional Brian was and, yes, scared. "Please try not to worry. I promise confidentiality and will contact you quickly."

Working his fingers under a collar that felt too tight, Brian wiped the sweat off his face and rubbed both hands with his handkerchief. "All right, but be quick about it. Thomas Chandler isn't going to sit on this long. No telling what he'll do. Do you think I should send my babies to their grandparents for awhile?"

"Do you have room for me to be a guest in your house for a short time?"

"I'll make room. I'll sleep with one of my children and you can have my room. What shall I tell Mrs. Morton? She'll naturally be curious as to why you're staying with us."

"Wait until I get there and we'll tell her together. It's only right that she is aware of the dangers and how it might effect her. Have you told her anything at all?"

"No. I was afraid she would become too frightened to stay with my babies."

"Well, don't say anything yet." Herb warned. "Be on the alert at home and while you're traveling. Give me you address and cell phone number, but I need to wait here and talk to the staff. The owner, Hannah Rutherford, may have other ideas."

"Oh, do you need to tell them about this?"

"I certainly do. They need to know where I am, and, too, you remember the old saying, 'two heads are better than one'. You met Victoria. Hey, here comes Hannah now."

Herb got up and walked to the door. "Hannah, do you have a few minutes to share with us?"

"Of course. Just let me put my packages down and take off my jacket. I'll be right there."

She came in and was introduced to Brian. Herb offered her a seat telling her it would take a few minutes. He let Brian tell his story and then played the tape for her. She was incensed.

"I am shocked and so angry. How dare this Tom character kill your wife and then try to take away your peace and freedom. Yes, I agree with Herb. He needs to be on the scene. Do you have someone you can trust to take Mrs. Morton and the babies?"

"Yes, many friends, but the ones I think of first are my wife's parents. They still keep in touch often because they loved their daughter and have treated me like their own son. They love the babies almost as much as I do. The only drawback is that they live in Richmond, Virginia."

"Hurrah! Does this Tom know about them?"

"Not to my knowledge."

"Do any of your neighbors know about them that might tell Tom if he asks where the children are?"

"I don't think any neighbor would remember them or even where they were from."

Herb jumped up. "Call them now and let me talk to them. The phone at your house might be bugged. We sweep through here often looking for bugs. So far, none."

With trembling hands Brian dialed the 703 area code and the number.

"Hello, Dad? Yes, it's Brian. I have a friend here -- oh, they're well and healthy. Growing like weeds. Hi, Mom. I'm glad you're on the extension. I have a life-saving favor to ask of you. I hope you're sitting down because the story is shocking and will make you very angry." He paused to listen.

"I want you to talk to this friend. He is a detective that I've hired to help me out of a dangerous situation."

Herb took the phone. "Hello, Mr. & Mrs. Sturgill. My name is Herbert Mueller. Call me Herb. I've been an MP in military and worked several years on the local police force. Now I'm with a lady in an investigation agency. We are angry for Brian and concerned for his safety and the safety of his babies. No Ma'am. The babies are fine at the present. The man giving Brian trouble has hinted that he can kill Brian's children if Brian doesn't cooperate with him. This would be better if we could talk face to face, but I'll try to be brief and give you the basic facts."

He proceeded to tell them Brian's story. "This is the man that killed Brian's wife -- your daughter. Now he's threatening Brian to get him to kill his, Tom's, wife. We need to get the babies and their nanny in a safe place for as long as it takes to get this man and keep everyone safe. Brian thought of you."

There was a pause while he listened to the distressed Sturgills talk.

Hannah motioned to give her the phone.

"Mr. & Mrs. Sturgill. My name is Hannah Rutherford. I am the lead investigator here and my father is a successful, law-abiding attorney. He will help me any time I need him.

I, too, was on the police force and still have a lot of respect from the Chief and patrolmen. In the meantime, I want to ask you please don't tell anyone that the babies will be with you. Mrs. Morton will come with them. If anyone asks just say the father is alone, still grieving, and very busy in his work. You are thrilled to have them visit you for awhile. I know that's true. Oh good, you're thrilled to help. Yes, we think Brian is innocent and needs a lot of help. I will personally bring Mrs. Morton and the babies up to you. I'll fill you in on all the details when I get there. Yes, here's Brian."

Brian took the phone. "Mom & Dad, I'd love to come with the babies, but I must not let anyone see me leave, especially with the children. We'll get together when this is over." He wiped his eyes. "Yes, we'll have our own prayer meeting. Thank you. I need a lot of prayer. I'll be in touch soon. When I call next, I'll just say the package you wanted will be delivered on such and such a day. Please don't talk about any of this on my phone at home or my cell phone. Herb and Hannah will be in touch. I love you, too. You know I do. God bless you both. Bye now."

Brian left feeling more relieved. Hannah called Victoria in. "Victoria, lock the front door and cut off the front lights, please. Come in Herb's office."

Victoria was as shocked as they were at the audacity of Tom Chandler.

"What are you going to do?"

Hannah stood up. "I have some urgent business to take care of and then I'm going to drive to Richmond and take them up. You and Herb will have to cover the office while

I'm gone. I'll call Chief Wingate and tell him I've been called out of town on business and Herb will be tied up with a case. I'll ask him to send officers by frequently to heck on you. Now I need to get Beth and Connie in here and give her the news I have."

CHAPTER NINE

"Beth, can you and Connie come in around five this afternoon and I'll give you the lowdown? No, wait until you get here, but drive carefully."

She next dialed the church office. "Marcie, Hi. It's Hannah. Is Pastor Bill in? I need to talk to him. Well, catch him quickly before he gets out of the building. Thank you, Marcie. It's very important."

After a few seconds the phone was picked up at the church. "Hi, Pastor Bill. I'm sorry to cause you to return. But this is very important. I need for you to tell the prayer group that will meet tonight and also announce it to whomever it concerns. My agency needs a cover of serious prayer. Yes, the lives of some innocent babies are involved. I can't tell about the case, but this is one time we need a lot of prayer. I will be out of town for a few days and Herb will be undercover. We truly need a lot of prayer. Yes, I would love for you to pray with me now."

Hannah hung up confident that a lot of prayers would be following them and she bet the Sturgills had asked their church for prayer.

She read over some notes on cases and wrote a report. She then pushed a button on the phone to talk to Victoria.

"Victoria, why don't you take your lunch break? I ate a late breakfast and will go out after you return. No, don't hurry. I'll be here all afternoon. Oh, by the way, Beth Correli and Connie Ackerman will be coming in around five. When they get here, signal me and send them on back. Thanks."

Herb had gone to Brian's house with him to tell Mrs. Morton about Brian's concerns. She was worried about all of them and anxious to do whatever she could. She hurried to make sure of clean clothes for the children and gathered toys, books and items they would need.

Hannah's phone buzzed. "Yes, Victoria?"

"Ms. Correli and Ms. Ackerman are here."

"Please send then back. Thank you."'

Hannah stood up and walked to open her door. Looking out she found the two young women nearby. "Come in, please. Have a seat."

Beth breathed a loud sigh. "I'm so relieved to see you smiling. I was afraid you were calling us down here to give us bad news."

"No, my dear, just the opposite. During my investigation I found that your - uh - friend was keeping company with some bad guys; in fact the mob. He had borrowed money for gambling and couldn't pay it back. They forced him to collect from others to earn his way. Somewhere along the line he had kept money for himself. They were teaching him a lesson as an example to others. You had a guardian angel with you to not be with him when they found him."

"Then the police still don't know about Beth?" Connie asked nervously.

"Only the three of us know what you observed. I wanted to tell you in person how serious this is though. Some day, Beth, you may tell your grandchildren about it, but in the meantime, keep it among us three. The mob could still come after you for fear you could identify them."

Beth was so relieved that tears were rolling down her cheeks. Connie reached over and took her hand. "This is a great example of how prayer protects and works."

"You're right, Connie. I can't tell you about any of my other cases, but I would appreciate it if you both kept me and my clients in your prayers. Their situation is even more serious than yours."

"How can I pray for you then?" Beth looked baffled.

"Just pray that God will guard me and the work I'm doing."

Connie jumped up. "I was about to forget those bloody clothes. What will we do with them?"

"I can give them back to you or I can dispose of them. It might be better if I dispose of them and then there is no way they can be connected to you. I also advise you not to talk to each other about this. You never know who might be listening. Try to forget it and act as if it never happened."

"Oh, please," Beth hiccupped. "Excuse me. Take them. I don't want to look at them again. How much do I owe you?"

"Call it a love gift. It makes me angry to see or hear of cruelty in any form or to anyone -- or an animal."

Connie got out a checkbook. "No, please. You put in time and effort. We want to pay you."

"Donate what you wish to shelters for abused women and children. I don't want or need your money. Let me know if I can be any further service. Go with God and watch -- your -- tongue."

Hannah had talked to Mrs. Morton and made plans. Mrs. Morton would have everything ready and be prepared to leave by seven thirty the next morning. Hannah knew she had to get there to place the car seats for both babies in her car. She had leased a large van because her sedan would not have carried all that was necessary for the children.

Herb had packed his items and drove the van to Brian's house. They backed it into Brian's garage so no one could see what they were loading. The windows were tinted. Hannah would drive his car over the next morning and leave it for him.

Hannah got up at five thirty and decided to make a quick short run to limber up. She was jogging along enjoying the cool morning when she saw eighty-six year old Martha DeWitt being walked by her three year old black Rottweiller. Hannah smiled at the determined expression on Martha's face as the dog set the pace and pulled her along. The dog was muscular and adored Martha, however, he was quick to let others know that he had a purpose in life -- to guard Martha.

They were a few feet from Hannah and Martha was smiling at her ready to speak. The dog suddenly stopped with the hair rising on the back of his neck and his teeth showing. He was snarling with a deep throat sound.

Martha suddenly looked frightened and squeaked, "Hannah."

Hannah started to pick up her pace to get to Martha when the dog lunged toward the street and almost pulled Martha over. Hannah was close enough to grab his leash. She looked to see what was causing the dog to be so angry. Just in time she threw herself down on her face and yelled at Martha to get down.

A black car had pulled beside them, the passenger window was cracked open and a pistol was showing. A bullet whizzed over Hannah's head as the car sped away. The dog tried his best to go after the car and even drug Hannah off the curb and into the street before she could stop him.

"Contagious," Martha yelled. "Come back here."

When Hannah heard the dog's name she was laughing so hard she paid no attention to her cuts and bruises. "Contagious? Where did you get his name?"

Martha grabbed the leash and began to scold the dog. He slunk back to her with his head hanging low.

"Oh, don't scold him. He saved our lives. Good boy. You are such a good, brave boy," Hannah patted him and praised him. He perked up and looked to Martha to get praise. She slowly patted him and thanked him for protecting them.

"Did you know those bad men, Hannah? Why did they want to kill you?"

"No, I don't know them, nor did I recognize the car. I don't know what they had in mind. In my business you make enemies without knowing it sometimes."

"Why?"

"People who are bad don't want anyone checking up on them and finding out about them. Where did the name, Contagious, come from?"

"My son. He brought me this rascal when he was weaned and helped me train him. I do love him. My son said to own a dog is contagious and all my friends would want one, also. He was teasing, but I liked the name."

"Well, you can rest assured no one else will have the same name. Ouch!"

"My dear, you're hurt. Your knees are bleeding, and your chin."

"Just surface skin knocked off. I'll be okay. It's better than having a bullet in me. I think I'll go back home and clean up. It's nice to see you, Martha. Bye, Contagious and thank you," she laughed patting him on the head.

Limping back to her house, she took a shower and placed bandages on her cut knees. She left her chin uncovered because it had stopped bleeding. She dressed in green linen slacks and a lime green fuzzy sweater for the trip.

I'm going north in winter weather so I'd better wear boots and socks. I'll pack a couple of pant suits. No need of a dress because I won't be socializing. I'll just leave Mrs. Morton and the babies, check into a motel for the night and get an early start back.

She took gloves and a knit cap out of a dresser drawer and a heavy coat from the closet that she had not worn in years. Packing the pant suits she added underclothes and extra socks. After some thought she put a book in that she had wanted to read. *I may want something to read in the motel. I sure would love to know what the intention of the shooter was and who he's connected with and why.*

Checking the kitchen clock she saw it was six forty and needed to leave. She debated with herself about calling Herb and Brian and telling them what had happened and then decided to just go over there. She carefully looked up and down the street as she got in Herb's car. On the way to Brian's house she constantly looked in the rear view mirror and the side mirrors to see if she was being followed. She picked up her cell phone and called Chief Wingate at home to tell him what had happened to her.

"Hannah, are you nuts or just having a death wish? Why are you out driving around when you might be followed and shot?"

"Chief, calm down. I'm fine except for some painful cuts and bruises. I'm working on a case and will be out of town for three or four days. Please have someone check my house to make sure there are no break-ins. Herb is occupied in an undercover case which leaves Victoria alone in the office. I would appreciate it if you'd have officers go by the office every now and then in case Victoria needs help."

"I'll do all of that and even visit with Victoria myself. I wish you'd tell me what's going on."

"Sorry, friend. You know I can't discuss cases with anyone other than my staff. I'll see you as soon as I get back. I did try to talk my client into giving you the information but no sale. Bye now."

At Brian's she pulled Herb's car behind the house with Brian's car. The back door was opened for her as she got out of the car. She ran into the house and thankfully accepted a cup of coffee and a cinnamon roll. She hadn't taken time to eat and was hungry.

While Mrs. Morton was bringing last minute articles down, Hannah told Herb and Brian about the morning. Herb was angry and Brian was frightened.

"Are you sure it's going to be safe for you to take my family to Richmond? Suppose you're followed?"

"The van is in your garage isn't it?"

"Yes, of course."

"You put everything that we're taking including car seats didn't you?"

Herb placed a comforting hand on Brian's shoulder. "Yes, everything is in the van and it's well hidden. All we have to do is place food in that Mrs. Morton prepared and the cooler with ice in it is already in the van. We'll only have to put the babies' food items and medicines in and get your things out of my car and put them in the van. Brian we're sending them off with a lot of prayers. Hannah is an excellent driver. I don't anticipate any trouble for them."

"Hannah, I personally checked the tires, oil, gas and all features that you'll depend on while you drive. Call my cell phone as soon as you get to Richmond. Give my cell number to the Sturgills and tell them not to call here at the house. We don't know who might be listening in."

CHAPTER TEN

Brian hugged each baby and kissed their cheek. "Matthew, you be a little man and help the ladies by being very good and doing whatever they say. I love you. Reinata, you don't understand what's going on, but some day you will. Mrs. Morton," he hugged her, "stay safe. I can never repay you for what you're doing to keep my babies safe. God bless you and keep you."

"Sure and it's a fine day when babies can't stay in their own home and be with the daddy who loves them. I'm proud that you trust me with my little darlings. We'll be all right. Don't you worry about us."

Even with tinted windows, they were very careful to not be seen. Mrs. Morton sat on the cooler in the back and would remain there for the first twenty or twenty-five miles. Both babies were asleep, so a soft, light blanket was placed over them so they would not be seen. Hannah was driving as if she were the only one in the van.

Herb and Brian stayed inside the house while Hannah drove away just in case someone was watching his house. Brian wanted desperately to stand outside and watch the van as long as he could see it, but Herb convinced him to stay in and make it appear as if Hannah had just been visiting. Later Brian went outside, as if he were alone, and puttered around preparing the flower beds for colder weather. It was difficult for him to go about daily routines as if it were a normal day. His heart was so heavy at the thought that his babies might be in trouble.

Hannah drove as if she didn't have a care in the world. She got on N Main St on US 501 until she could drive on US 17 N. Here Mrs. Morton came up to sit with Hannah. She drove through Fayetteville, N.C. and on to Wilson where they stopped to change diapers, give Reinata a bottle and Matthew a sippy cup and pieces of apple. Hannah and Mrs. Morton took turn about using the restroom. Hannah bought a Diet Coke and a egg and sausage biscuit. Mrs. Morton bought coffee and a bagel. They bought gas.

Mrs. Morton took Matthew by the hand and let him walk around a little bit while Hannah had Reinata on her shoulder patting her back. They were beginning to feel the November cold as they traveled farther north.

In the van, and ready to go again, Hannah looked with concern at Mrs. Morton. "Are you going to be able to adjust to such an abrupt change in weather? It's cool, but not this cold in South Carolina."

"Yes, my dear, I'm prepared. I purchased warmer clothing for the wee ones and I think I can get by with what I have. Anyway, Mr. Brian gave me too much money if I needed it. I shall pay our way with the grandparents, but be careful not to waste it."

By the time they were going around Norfolk, Virginia, it was really cold. Matthew was wide-eyed constantly asking "Whatat?" They patiently answered him so that he would know what he was seeing. He finally yelled, "Down!"

"Do you need to potty?" Mrs. Morton asked him. He nodded his head so hard Hannah could not understand why he didn't hurt. Hannah pulled over going around Petersburg and Mrs. Morton took him to a restroom for his business.

Both women praised him for being a little man and he was so proud of himself. He wanted something to eat. Hannah pulled over at a fast food place and got a plain hamburger and French fries which he only ate half of each and a few bites of a banana.

It was getting dusky, and Hannah pulled over to call the Sturgills on her cell phone to tell them they were almost there. "We're going to stop and it looks as if we'll be there about seven."

"You will not stop," Mrs. Sturgill said emphatically. I have a good supper ready for you. I know the babies will need to be fed, bathed and put down for the night. I've borrowed two cribs for them and have two rooms ready for you ladies. We can hardly wait to see you. Hurry on in -- but be careful."

Hannah was grateful that she had been able to make the trip in such a short time. There was little traffic and she did drive fast on the interstates.

She said a prayer of thanks as they pulled into the Sturgill's driveway.

David and Amanda Sturgill ran out to meet them. They each took a baby. Reinata slept on in her grandmother's arms, but Matthew came wide awake when his grandfather took him. Suddenly Matthew pointed up and yelled, "At"

"What does he want?" David asked.

"He's saying, 'what's that?'" Hannah explained. "Sweetheart, that's snow."

"No."

"S s s snow," she repeated.

"At?" he asked again.

"Something very cold and we need to get in. Come on, ladies, I'll take what you need out tonight and will get the rest tomorrow."

Hannah and Mrs. Morton were thankful to get in out of the cold air and know they had arrived safely. Hannah immediately called Herb.

"Hey, buddy. The packages arrived safely and they're all in good shape."

"I'm so relieved. My friend has made a quick run to get some items. I didn't think he should go out, but --. He's an adult and he has been so antsy. He'll be delighted to know everything arrived in good shape. Talk to you soon."

Mrs. Morton and Amanda Sturgill together fed the children, bathed them and got them in bed. Then the adults sat down for David to ask a blessing. The Virginia ham, gravy, biscuits, mashed potatoes, green beans, pickled beets, deviled eggs and Martha Washington pie were devoured gratefully. In fact, Hannah ate more than she was accustomed to eating it was all so good. She offered to wash the dishes and clean up, but was pushed into the den to talk and answer questions about what was happening in Brian's house. She kept yawning and apologizing. She was ashamed to be awakened later and followed the suggestion that she go to bed.

Amanda asked Mrs. Morton to stay and tell her more about the children and what she knew of the happenings.

"I wish you would call me Amanda," she stated. "We're going to be together for some time. My heart is so full of fear and love for this little family. It broke our hearts when our daughter died and now to find she was actually murdered! Poor Brian. We do love him." David nodded. "We love him because he loved our daughter and was so good to her. We know how much he grieved and how much he loves the babies." She sighed.

David broke in. "Please call us David and Amanda."

"I shall be glad to if you'll call me Alicia."

They talked until all of them were yawning and tired. David stood. "Forgive us, Alicia. You've had a long, tiring trip and have had a lot of worries and responsibilities. We are more grateful than I can find words to express myself. Go to bed and sleep as late as you like. We'll take care of our grandchildren."

Hannah woke to the wonderful odors of bacon and coffee. She stretched lazily and then was horrified to discover that it was nine o'clock. She jumped up, grabbed a change of clothes and ran across the hall for a hot shower.

David greeted her with a hug and a kiss on the cheek. "I hope you slept well and are rested. You had a lot on your shoulders and I'm sure you're still exhausted."

Amanda stepped out of the kitchen to give her a firm hug. "We just can't tell you enough how much we appreciate you. Sit down and have a good breakfast."

Hannah looked with horror at the plate Amanda placed in front of her. First there was orange juice and coffee. The plate held scrambled eggs, four slices of bacon and two biscuits. A gravy boat was on the side with good old fashioned milk gravy.

"Whoa. Thank you so much, but I never eat this much at breakfast and I had such a big supper that I'm ashamed of myself." She turned to return Matthew's cheerful, "Hi!" from his high chair.

Reinata was looking pleased with herself with a big, gummy grin. This was her first experience to sit in a high chair. She had always been in an infant carrier, but Amanda felt the baby was big enough for her own chair. She spread her mouth in a big grin when Hannah laughed. Matthew beat on the tray and laughed loudly thinking they were having a great time.

"Hoooo," David moaned, holding his ears. "I had forgotten that part of child rearing. Our daughter used to beat on the tray and try to sing loudly."

"She must have been a wonderful little girl," Hannah stated. She thanked Mrs. Morton as she handed her a cloth napkin.

"She was the best baby. Of course we thought so, but everyone who knew us commented on what a good baby she was. She never gave us any trouble growing up," Amanda added.

Hannah patted her stomach. "The food here is so delicious you're going to have trouble getting rid of me. I've appreciated it and certainly enjoyed it."

David laughed. "No one is running you off. We would love for you to stay as long as you like."

"Thank you. That's sweet of you," she said reaching to take the hand Reinata was waving at her. "I have clients who are depending on me and I have no choice. I must return home today.

"Look outside," Amanda said smiling. "I don't think you're going any where, at least for today. Just be patient.

This will be over by late afternoon and you can leave in the morning if you're determined to go."

The snow was falling so thick and fast that it seemed impossible to see through the white curtain falling. Hannah gave an exclamation of disgust and used her napkin to wipe her mouth.

"How in the world do you live in this and survive the winters? I would be stir crazy in a short time."

David laughed. "We're used to it; besides it never lasts long. If the meteorologists inform us of a possible lengthy snow storm, we hurry out, like everyone else, and stock up on items we'll need."

Amanda added, "Yes, we even stocked up on firewood in case we had to use the fireplace for heat. And I have cast iron skillets and a cast iron Dutch oven in case I need to cook over the fireplace."

"Wow. I didn't stop to think. Of course you're prepared. I would be sure to stock up on reading material," Hannah laughed.

Hannah made a quick call to Herb. "Packages much appreciated. Need to be involved a day or two longer due to weather. All is well."

CHAPTER ELEVEN

Back home in Myrtle Beach Hannah thought she would never be warm again. She moaned to Victoria, "How can any one live in that as long as they do? It is beautiful and I enjoyed it for a few minutes, but my blood is too thin from the warm weather and I could not adjust quickly. Maybe after living there a few years-----," she laughed.

Victoria laughed. "I was born and grew up in Minnesota. You don't know cold until you've experienced winter there. My two brothers stayed there. They're both doctors and doing well. My father is still there, but all three of us are trying to get him to move down here. When I came down for college I knew this is where I belong. My mother died five years ago."

"Well, I'm eternally grateful that you did stay. I could not get along without you. Are there messages for me or something I need to be working on?"

"Yes, and I want to thank you for asking the Chief to send officers to check on me. A few even came in to keep me company sometimes. One has been coming back often and we've developed a nice friendship."

"Oh, really! And who might this special officer be?"

"I don't think you know him. He's only been working about seven months. His name is Liam O'Brien. He has such beautiful wavy black hair and I truly think he's kissed the Blarney Stone, only he's not Irish."

"Huh. What is he then with a name like that?"

"His mother came from a country in Africa and was a very light- skinned black. His father is Irish. His mother's father was from Holland, so he's quite a mixture of races. Does it matter?"

"Of course not. You know I judge people by their character and I assume you do the same. If you're happy, then I'm happy. I trust you to use common sense. Don't forget the wonderful plans you have for your future. Be very sure that whomever you choose will understand your dreams and desires and will respect them."

"At the present we're just good friends. I want you to meet him and judge for yourself."

Hannah stood up. "Right now I'm anxious to hear from Herb and hear if there are any developments in Mr. Harmon's case." She went back to her office to call Herb.

"Hey gorgeous. I'm glad you called. I'm having the time of my life. I've found a Cribbage player who enjoys the game as much as I do. We've found we like the same CDs and mostly the same television programs. But that isn't why you called. I don't think he's found that I'm staying here. By now he's probably learned that Brian is alone. The phone will ring but no one talks when Brian answers."

"Don't you have a tracer on the phone?"

"Yes. The calls are coming from various pay phones over town or from prepaid phone cards that can't be traced. One day Brian went to Office Depot for supplies for his writing. He hadn't been gone long until someone rang the doorbell. I kept very quiet, but then had to jump and hide behind a chair in the living room because the person put his face up to the window to try to see inside. I could hear him chuckle and then I heard footsteps going all around the house. When Brian came home there was a paper stuck to the garage door saying 'Caught you'."

"Good grief. What did he mean by that?"

"I've no idea. I guess he's just trying to play on Brian's nerves."

"Has Brian agreed for you to talk to his pastor?"

"Not yet, but he's getting there. I think I've convinced him that he needs someone on his side that can go to court and be believed if it comes to that."

"Okay. I really called to see if we can get together for Thanksgiving. Let me know today and I'll make reservations at the Cypress Room. I always eat with daddy, but he'll be glad to join us."

Hannah went out to ask Victoria if she had plans for Thanksgiving and found a tall, very handsome deputy talking to her.

"Hannah, I'm glad you walked out here. I want you to meet Liam O'Brien who has been making sure I'm safe while you were gone."

"Hello, Liam," Hannah said walking to shake his hand. "I'm so glad to meet you and want to thank you for looking after my dear friend here."

"It was my pleasure, Miss Rutherford. We were told to make sure your office was protected."

"And Victoria came with it," Hannah laughed. He blushed.

"Victoria, I really came out to see if you had plans for Thanksgiving. I've just been talking to Herb and we're going to try to get together for a meal."

"We were just talking about that, Miss Rutherford."

"Liam, stop that. Please call me Hannah. Well, would the two of you like to join us at the Cypress Room? It will be on me because I like to treat my staff for special occasions."

"I would love to join you, Miss R - er, Hannah, but you don't have to pay for me."

"Shush. No more of that. If you come as a member of our party, than you're one of us. Then I can count on you two?"

Victoria and Liam looked at each other, grinned and nodded.

"Hooray. Thank you." Hannah left and went back to her office to call her daddy. He, of course, accepted. She promised to call him later with particulars.

The six of them; Hannah and her father, Andrew Rutherford, Brian Harmon, Herb Mueller, Victoria Stallard and Liam O'Brien gratefully gathered around a table to share Thanksgiving. Andrew asked a blessing and they passed the family style dishes around. Turkey, stuffing, dressing, candid sweet potatoes, potato salad, broccoli, snow peas, glazed carrots and rolls. Coffee, iced tea, or soft drinks were offered and hot cider came after the meal. Choice of pumpkin pie, mince pie or apple pie was offered. Everyone chose pumpkin, some with whipped cream.

Herb left the table first to drive to Brian's house and park two blocks down. He came along the alley and in the back door. In that manner, if anyone was watching Brian's house, Brian would be seen coming home alone.

Two days after Thanksgiving, Herb and Brian were awakened, at two fifteen in the morning, by loud bangs on the front door. Herb held a pistol in his hand but stayed back out of sight while Brian eased to the door. He looked out carefully, but could see no one. He finally opened the door, holding his foot at the bottom so he could shut it quickly. No one. He opened the door fully and found a hatchet stuck in the door.

"Don't touch it," Herb spoke. "If we're lucky there'll be fingerprints on it." Herb still stayed back out of sight because he was sure someone was out there staying out of sight just to observe Brian's reaction. Brian kept himself as calm as possible. Holding a table napkin, he worked the hatchet out of the door and stepped back inside, locking the door behind him.

Shades were kept down at night, or when lights were on in the house, so that one could not see into the house through the windows.

Brian was shaking as he laid the hatchet on the dining room table. "I'm so thankful my babies are not here in the house. If they were here, and in danger, I would not be able to think about myself."

Herb finally convinced Brian to let him call a friend of his who was a detective on the city police force. Regardless of the time of night, Herb called Alan Turner and ask him to come to Brian's house. Alan was driving an unmarked car and wearing jeans, a sweatshirt and a denim jacket. Any one observing would just see a friend coming in. Herb called Hannah.

Alan was shocked and angry when he heard the entire story and saw the hatchet. "Mr. Harmon, with your permission I'm going to start a search of records on Thomas Chandler."

Brian was frightened and concerned. "Officer Turner, I've hesitated to bring this before the police for -- well frankly --I don't know whom I can trust. Too, I wasn't sure they would feel there was enough to be concerned about. But now he's showing that he means business."

"He's showing he's a psychopath and very dangerous. We need to stop him before he involves innocent people and makes the situation much worse and heartbreaking. Mr. Mueller has done the right thing by staying with you, but keeping hidden. As long as Chandler thinks you're in a hopeless, helpless situation, he'll be more inclined to act where he can be apprehended. Hopefully before he kills his own wife," Turner stated.

Hannah leaned forward. "Officer Turner, do you think we should inform his wife and maybe warn her in some way?"

"I don't know the woman. She might listen to you and she might resent you and decide to work against you. Let me have her observed, talk quietly to neighbors, friends, or whomever we can find. We need to build a profile of her, also. We don't even know if she'll believe us. It must be done subtly, so that Chandler is not feeling that he is being pushed in a corner and acts in an irrational manner. Please allow me to handle her."

"In other words this is going to take time, and we must stay low key and be patient," Herb stated.

"Well spoken. This is not the movies where a crime is solved in an hour. Be prepared for it to be days or even weeks."

Brian moaned, "I miss my babies and it isn't fair to me or them that we must be separated. Thank God for wonderful in-laws. I love them dearly. They feel the same about me and my children."

Hannah stood up. "In the meantime, we do have other clients and obligations to others. A prestige law firm has hired me to do some important research for them. That, too, cannot be accomplished overnight. Eventually it might mean I must make some short trips out of town. I've come to the conclusion that I must hire more detectives. I don't hire just anyone that appears interested. I have the Sheriff investigate them thoroughly. We need qualified helpers, not wannabes. Thank you for including me tonight and I will be available for any assistance I can give. I hate to give Herb up for an indeterminable amount of time, but it is necessary. Good night everyone. Stay safe and have faith."

Brian, Herb and Alan continued talking and making plans for the most safe, feasible way to trap Thomas Chandler without violence or involving an innocent person.

Alan finally stood and yawned broadly, stretching his arms and arching his back. "Sorry, fellows, but I'm really tired. This must be a sure clue to old age because I used to go all night and work the next day. Of course Uncle Sam put a kink in that when he took me in the Army and sent me off to help win the Gulf Storm. Yeah, sure. You know how much winning I did? Just the same as all the other poor sleezers."

Herb jumped up and thumped Alan on the back giving him a manly hug. "I just can't thank you enough for coming out on such short notice and in the dead of night. Remember, we're trying to keep this as low key as possible."

"Please accept my gratitude and know you're welcome here any time," Brian said sluggishly.

Alan laughed. "I know someone else who needs to go to bed. Good night and try not to worry. We'll work this out in a safe, legitimate way."

Herb stayed back out of sight while Brian closed the door and locked it. He and Herb again checked that all doors and windows were locked, the alarm was set and shades were drawn. Then they went to their own rooms and prepared to get some rest.

CHAPTER TWELVE

The December air in Myrtle Beach, South Carolina was pleasant ranging from low to middle sixties. Hannah started out on her early morning run admiring the magenta sunrise. In spite of all that happened, she still didn't feel that she was in a great deal of danger.

Thinking about the investigative work she was doing for a prestigious law firm, and of Brian Harmon's problems, she didn't hear a runner coming rapidly behind her. Without warning she was tackled from behind and an arm came around her throat. A raspy voice, obviously faked, reminded her that she was butting into something that didn't concern her.

Desperately trying to talk, she strangled out, "I don't know what you're talking about. What do you mean?"

A harsh laugh answered her, but suddenly the man was up and gone, running across a neighbor's lawn and to a back alley. A hand helped her up and a concerned voice asked her what was going on.

Hannah blearily looked into the face of a police officer. "I just happened to be driving down this street and saw in the distance that a man in a hooded sweat suit had someone on the ground. It looked like a fight so I picked up speed and he ran when he saw me coming." The officer looked concerned and angry.

"I don't know who he was. Didn't get to look at him because he stayed at my back. It was unexpected and I didn't have time to defend myself. Did you see what he looked like?" Hannah chocked.

"No, I'm sorry. The hood was up until I couldn't see anything. I could just see he was a big man, not fat, just big. Much too big to be attacking you. Do you have an enemy, or have you been receiving threats?"

"No. Oh, wait. Several weeks ago I had a late night phone call which stated that I should stay out of things that were none of my business if I wanted to live and if I wanted my staff safe."

"Your staff?"

"Yes. I own and operate the Lost Cause Detective Agency."

"Oh, yes. I've heard of you. Didn't you, at one time, work as a police officer on our city force?"

"Yes, but to the best of my knowledge, I didn't make any enemies while I worked there. I left with everyone liking me and willing to work with me." She gave a weak laugh. "At least to my face."

"I've heard nothing but good about you. Let me help you. Why don't you get in the car and I'll drive you home, or do you need to go to the hospital?"

"Thanks ever so much, but I'll turn that kind offer down. I don't intend to be intimidated, especially in my own town, and I'll not allow him to see me appearing to be weak."

"That's not being weak, it's being sensible. He may be hiding around somewhere watching us and waiting for another chance at you."

"What is, is and I'll carry on. Thanks for the hand up, but I'll be going on." She smiled at him and skipping backwards gave a little wave before turning and running on.

The officer shook his head. "That's one gutsy lady. I sure hope she'll be okay. Well, whether she likes it or not, I'll have to write a report on this."

Hannah returned home, took a shower and decided to eat breakfast. She drank a glass of orange juice, scrambled two eggs and fried two slices of bacon. Leaving the bacon on a paper towel to drain, she placed bread in the toaster. Just as she had finished and stood up to rinse the dishes and place them in the dishwasher, the phone rang.

"Good morning," she sang out thinking it was one of her staff calling.

"Have you gotten the message yet or will we have to use harsh methods?"

Her temper hit the ceiling. "Listen, you creep. I've done nothing that I'm ashamed of or against anyone else. If you weren't such a coward you'd face me and tell me what you're so disturbed over. I know a couple of good psychiatrists that will be glad to help you."

She grumbled when the phone was slammed in her ear. "Well, hoop-te-do. If you didn't like what I had to say, why don't you come talk to me, or better still LET ME ALONE." she screamed out.

She finished cleaning the kitchen, brushed her teeth and went to work.

Victoria and Herb were angry when they heard Hannah's story.

"How long has this been going on? Why haven't you told me about this before?" Herb raved.

"I can't do any fighting, but I sure can scream bloody murder. I would love to be around sometime when this miserable character shows up." Victoria shook with angry.

Herb looked disbelieving at her. "What good would screaming do?"

"It would call attention to what was going on, and hopefully cause the perpetrator to run off." She snapped.

"I love you both for caring and don't want to involve either one of you. I'll do what has to be done and hope for the best. By the way, Victoria, the baddies are no longer called perpetrator. They are now called the unsubs meaning unknown subjects."

"Live and learn," Victoria snapped, flinging her hair as she turned quickly to go to her desk.

Herb placed an arm around Hannah and walked her to her office. "Are you sure you aren't hurt? A tackle can cause a lot of damage. Ask any football player. Remember your own tackle some months ago."

'I've been bruised before and will again. No. Thank you for caring, but I'm all right. I just need to be more alert from now on. Sheesh. In my own hometown." With a sigh of disgust, she started on some written reports.

"I've got to get back to Brian's before that Chandler fellow shows up again. Brian won't admit it, but he's afraid to be alone now, and I can't blame him. Call me on my cell if you need me."

Herb parked two blocks below Brian and started walking up the alley. As he came within sight of Brian's house, he saw a man sneaking down the alley and going through the back gate. Herb quickly and quietly ran to the area and looked over the fence. He saw the man was almost to the house and carrying something in his hand. Herb quickly called 9-1-1 on his cell phone and asked for emergency help. "He may have a bomb of some sort for all I know."

Just as the man drew back his hand to throw what really was a homemade bomb, Herb yelled at him and ran toward him. The man ran around the house to the front and right into the arms of the police. These two officers had been in the neighborhood and others were coming behind them.

It wasn't Thomas Chandler, but after several hours of questioning the man broke and admitted that Chandler had hired him to throw the bomb. "It was just to set the house on fire at the back."

Herb stooped down to get in the man's face. "Are you aware that this man, that lives there, has two small children? One is three and one is a year old."

The poor man looked as if he would faint. "No. I didn't know there were babies in the house. I was told that this man had borrowed money and refused to pay it back. The bomb was supposed to scare him, that's all. I swear it."

"For your information, you were told a complete lie. This man has not borrowed money, nor has he had any business dealings with Chandler. The truth is that Chandler committed a serious crime and this man knew about it. Chandler is afraid he'll tell on him and get him arrested." Herb was angry.

"Give us your name, address and phone number. We'll have to decide what to do with you," one officer told him.

"My full name is Harold Alvin McComber. I live at 335 Pine Ave. in Garden City. I'm a fool. I have a ten year old son who needs a liver transplant. I can't afford the cost and want to do what I can to keep my son alive. My wife is working also and her heart is breaking because we have four children and no money. Chandler came into the restaurant where I work and heard one of the other waiters ask me about my son. I told him how worried we were because we needed money that I couldn't get. He came to me after work as I left the restaurant and told me that this man owed him two hundred thousand dollars and refused to pay it back. The bomb was a weak one he made and he said it would not cause much damage, but would scare him into paying what he owed. He offered me fifty thousand dollars for the job. I was not to hurt anyone, just cause a fire that could easily be put out. How am I going to explain this to my poor, sweet wife and children? I even sing in my church choir. How can I explain to my church why I would do such a thing? I needed the money for my son's medical needs." By now he was crying.

Brian and Herb felt sorry for him, but he did attempt to damage property with the chance of causing bodily harm.

Officer Fred Morrison felt badly, also, but he had a duty to perform. "I'm sorry, sir, but I have to take you in. First I need to remind you that you have the right to remain silent. Anything you say can and will be used against you in a court of law. You also have the right to an attorney. If you can't afford an attorney, one will be provided for you by the court. Do you understand these rights?"

"Yes, I do. Thank you. I've never been arrested, but I've watched police shows on television and know pretty much what goes on. I also have the right to a phone call. As much as I hate to do it, I must call my wife and tell her where I am. She'll worry if she doesn't hear from me and now she'll be heartbroken."

Herb placed an arm around Harold's shoulders. "If you sign a statement, and have it notarized, telling all that Chandler asked you to do, it will go easier on you. We have tried to get him in a place where he has to face officers of the court for some time. You will be a big help to us if you're willing to testify against him."

"Yes, of course, I'll be glad to do it. He lied to me and put me in a position to get into real trouble. I'll be glad to cooperate."

Herb grinned with relief. "Sgt. Morrison, we're so glad you're hearing this. Please take good care of this man. Take his statement and then please send two men to bring Thomas Chandler in for questioning. Be careful for he's a slippery customer. He's too smart for his own good. But he's proven to be a psychopath."

"I shall be delighted to do that," Fred Morrison agreed. "I'll bring the Chief up-to-date as soon as I take Mr. McComber's statement. We'll send two officers to, hopefully, get him out of bed and bring him in. With all Mr. Harmon has told us and now this gentleman, we should be able to take Mr. Chandler before a judge quickly."

They said their goodbyes and Sgt. Morrison left with his prisoner. Herb didn't feel that he should leave Brian yet. Chandler might get away from them and come after Brian.

Or he may have hired someone else to do damage. It would not be safe to leave Brian yet.

Herb called Hannah to tell her of the happenings. She was as thrilled as the men were. "I'm relieved that you arrived in time to stop the fire bombing. You're right. Stay with Brian until this is completely cleared."

CHAPTER THIRTEEN

Hannah reluctantly made preparations to drive down to Tallahassee, Florida and get copies of some records for the attorneys for whom she was working.

Not realizing how long it might take, she packed enough clothing for three days. Again she told Chief Wingate that she would appreciate someone checking on the office and on Victoria while she was gone. "I hope I'm not gone more than three days, but one never knows."

She then called Herb and asked if he needed her for several days. He was doing fine and was ecstatic that Chandler was arrested and the case was building against him. Chandler had obtained a high-priced attorney, James Shipero, who had a reputation for getting even the guilty free of charges. Herb felt that all the evidence would be sufficient to convict Chandler. The prosecution was asking for a psychiatrist to give Thomas Chandler a complete test for mental stability, and for standing trial.

"The prosecution is asking for a complete psychiatric examination, and they'll get it." Herb chortled. "This is one trial I'm going to enjoy attending." He felt a little ashamed to talk on when Hannah was having to work away from home.

"Hannah, be very careful. Stop at night before it gets dark and stay where there's a lot of light and traffic, preferably one with a good restaurant, also." He laughed. "You might know I'd think of food first."

"I'll be careful. I will carry my pistol, but, after all, I'm going to a very civilized city, and, I'm sure, there are thousands of good, honest people there." She laughed.

"I know. You're not going into the wilds of the jungle, but criminals do live everywhere. Keep in touch. I'll worry if I don't hear from you."

"Herb, what is going to happen to that poor Mr. McComber who was just trying to get money to make sure his son had the surgery?"

"Brian asked the officer to let him leave as he was not going to press charges against him, but the officer said he would have to keep him overnight and take him before a judge tomorrow. The judge would hear the facts and take Brian's offer into consideration."

"Oh, good. I've been worried about him." She giggled. "He'll think twice after this before he does something like that again. I bet, from now on, he'll be very careful to consult others before he jumps at what seems like a good chance. He should remember, 'if it sounds too good to be true it probably is".

"I'm sure he will. Hannah, please be careful and let me know how you're doing."

"I will. Be seeing you, Herb. Give Brian my best wishes."

Hannah had set her alarm for six o'clock, Tuesday morning. She checked again to make sure she wasn't forgetting something she would need. She showered and dressed in a pink pull-over fairly dressy blouse and lilac slacks with lilac- colored shoes.

Once more checking her 38 Smith and Wesson and picking up a box of additional hollow-point bullets, she put in a pad of paper with notes for her assignment on it and the letters of introduction from the attorneys. All of this went in a briefcase that would be with her at all times.

She placed her suitcase in the truck of her light blue Camry and the briefcase on the front seat. She ran back for a light jacket just in case she might need it. She had gotten trip books from AAA and planned her driving directions. She knew it was five hundred one miles to Tallahassee and would take close to nine hours if she drove straight through. She planned on enjoying the countryside and stopping along if she so desired.

At seven o' clock she left her home and got on U.S. 17 to drive south. She drove to Mount Pleasant and decided to stop for breakfast. She was fascinated with the name of the restaurant, MELLOW MUSHROOM.

Inside she found friendly servers and a wonderful ambience.

Although Hannah, as a general rule, did not eat a big breakfast, she decided to eat hearty because she didn't know what she might find on the road. She ordered orange juice, decaf, one scrambled egg, which came with mushrooms, one piece of crisp bacon and one pancake. She was embarrassingly full, but did order a second cup of coffee.

While she drank her coffee, she perused the AAA material on Mount Pleasant.

Boone Hall Plantation & Gardens -- Hannah had heard so much about this lovely old place that traced its land grant to 1681 to Major John Boone.

There were formal gardens and authentic cabins. She read that a visitor should allow three hours to cover the house and grounds. No time for that. She determined to return some day for a tour.

She continued to read. Oysters, blue crabs and shrimp are brought in fresh daily. South Carolina is known for good food, especially seafood. Some of the natives still speak Gullah, a lyrical mixture of old English and African languages. Old St. David's Church, built before the Revolution, has been well cared for and is a beautiful tourist attraction.

Shipwrecks from 1514 can be located in the coastal waters where the Spanish explored. Superb golf courses, and excellent year around weather, are famous in South Carolina with some world champion golfers enjoying the links.

In 1521 Francisco Gordillo explored the coast and wrote glowing reports on it. In 1670 Charles Town became the first permanent English settlement. In 1788 South Carolina was recognized as the eighth state. In 1861 Fort Sumter was attacked and began the War Between The States, In 1989 Hurricane Hugo did dreadful damage. In 1996 the Supreme Court ruled that females could be admitted to the previously all male military schools.

In 2005 the Arthur Ravenel, Jr. Bridge was opened which connected Charleston and Mount Pleasant. In 1786 the capital was moved from Charleston to Columbia.

Hannah was known for dedication to duty, so, she continued south on Hwy. 17 and soon found she was in Georgia. She loved reading about the history of cities and states, but she didn't have time to sit and dream.

She decided to go through Athens and avoid the traffic and people in Atlanta. Here she stopped to get gas. While she was there she got some cheese on cheese crackers and a Diet Cola. Pulling off and parking on one side of the parking lot, she read the AAA book on Georgia. *Wow! What a big book and what a lot of information. All of the states have a lot of interesting history, but Georgia seems to have a great deal.*

On April 21, 1732, King George signed a charter for a state that was to be named for him. In thirty years Georgia will celebrate its tercentenary or 360 years. In the early 1800s, nineteen rich blacks came from Africa and purchased land. Some of them developed large plantations with slaves.

In 1777 Savannah became the first capital. Thirteen cities later, in 1868, Atlanta became the capital and is today. Margaret Mitchell lived in Atlanta when she wrote "Gone With The Wind." Fifteen miles south of Atlanta is a beautiful plantation. In 1839 a Greek Revival house, Stately Oaks, was built and was used as Tara during the movie.

Ten miles south of Savannah is the Wormsloe Plantation, built by Noble Jones in 1730 and has remained in the family of descendents today. He planted mulberry trees hoping to have silk worms and start a silk industry.

The descendants didn't try as hard to improve or develop the plantation. The name, Wormsloe came from their hometown in Wales.

Plains is the home of our 39th President, Jimmy Carter. Andersonville has a lot of history; the main one seems to be the awful prison that caused the death and injuries of so many military men during the War Between The States.

Ashburn is known for its big crop of peanuts, called goober peas.

Hannah realized time was rushing by, and if she sat and read, she'd be there the next morning. She reluctantly laid the book on the seat beside her and carefully pulled out into what was now rush-hour traffic. She headed south toward Macon

She wasted no more time driving on to Albany and pulled into the area around Tallahassee, Florida just at dusk. Victoria had made reservations for her at a La Quinta Inn just minutes from the state capital in Tallahassee. She checked in, walked to the restaurant next door and ate a light supper before going to her room for a shower and an early night. She was very tired from driving all day. Tomorrow would be a busy day when she went to the city courthouse to find the information the attorneys wanted.

Wednesday morning dawned bright, clear and a little cool. Hannah dressed in a lime green suit with a yellow blouse and yellow shoes with a low heel. She didn't know how much she would be standing and walking and didn't want hurting feet.

She stopped in the lobby for an European breakfast that was offered free to guests. There was juice, coffee, bagel with cream cheese or a Danish, fresh fruit and hot or cold cereal. She selected an orange juice, decaf, a bagel with cream cheese and a small slice each of honeydew, cantaloupe and watermelon with three fresh strawberries. She smiled to learn the strawberry growing season in Florida was late November through the last of March.

She returned to her room to freshen and brush her teeth. She checked her briefcase for the necessary work and then called Herb to report that she had arrived and all was well. It was such a nice morning that she decided to walk.

La Quinta was on 2905 North Monroe and the Leon County courthouse was on 301 South Monroe. No trouble, but if she found it too tiresome to walk, she could flag a cab. She walked briskly enjoying the clean, fresh air and the fact that everyone she met was smiling at her.

It was a long walk, but Hannah enjoyed it. She made her way through a group of people who seemed to be congregating for some specific purpose and went into the courthouse.

The young woman at the receptionist desk was looking apprehensively at the crowd outside the door. Hannah looked back and then at the young woman. "Is there a possibility of trouble?"

The young woman quickly apologized and welcomed Hannah. "No trouble. I hope. My husband is one of the officers on duty out there and I'm always afraid that someone in a crowd will get out of control and cause a fight or even pull a gun."

"Why are they out there?" Hannah asked curiously.

"There are some people who never agree with the method used to evaluate their property for tax purposes. Those are demanding that our tax authorities all be removed from office and others installed. Zeesh. They don't realize how much more money that would cost. Besides, whoever is elected, there will be some still protesting. You can't please them all. It's interesting that the ones protesting are the ones who really don't have much or are not paying much at all."

"As long as there are people on this earth there will be someone protesting something," Hannah smiled.

"Oh, I'm sorry," the young woman suddenly looked ashamed. "I was so worried about my husband and not paying attention to my business. How may I assist you?"

"My name is Hannah Rutherford. I need to speak to someone about information on property ownership."

"Do you have a complaint?"

"No. Thankfully. I'm here on business for a client." She held out her badge and identification card.

"Oh, my goodness. I'll call Ginny Grogan and ask her to assist you. Please have a seat and she'll be out here in a few minutes."

"Thank you." Hannah walked to a very comfortable light brown leather chair and appreciated it. She checked again to make sure all the papers she would need were in her briefcase. She knew they were there, but it was a nervous habit to keep checking.

In just three or four minutes a lady came bustling to her. She smiled at a woman possibly in her middle fifties, short, but stylish pepper and salt hair, about five four and around one fifty. The woman was smiling and holding out a hand to shake hands with Hannah.

"Hello, I'm Virginia Grogan. Call me Ginny. And how may I help you?"

"I'm Hannah Rutherford," she said showing her badge and I D card. "Could we go somewhere private and talk? I have a very private business nature."

"Certainly. Please come with me."

The two ladies walked through a security gate, down a short hall and into a room that appeared to be a conference room. A long table, eight comfortable chairs and a smaller table with beverages, pastries, napkins and everything necessary on it were all that was in the room.

"Please have a seat," Ginny offered Hannah. "Would you like something to drink, or snack?"

"Thank you, no. Is there an attorney in the building, or one near, that is familiar with your work and can join us?"

Ginny looked quizzically at Hannah. "You want an attorney present?"

"Yes, please. We'll need one, preferably one that is familiar with property laws and property tax laws."

Ginny stood up slowly and said, "Excuse me. Yes, I know the very one to call." She left the room and was back in about five minutes. "Attorney James Bridges will join us in a few moments. In the meantime, would you like to tell me what this is about?"

"I could, but then I'd have to tell Mr. Bridges and you'd hear the same story twice. How long will it be before Mr. Bridges joins us?"

"He's upstairs, but he's on a long distance phone call and I don't really know how long he will be. He knows we're waiting, so, he won't keep us waiting long."

CHAPTER FOURTEEN

Hannah smiled. "I'm curious as to what the group out front hopes to accomplish."

"Pay no attention. As long as they just march, wave signs and talk, there's no problem, except they're in the way of people entering on legitimate business. There's always some group stirred up about something. I feel sorry for the police officers who are assigned to just be out there and make sure there is no trouble. Where are you from, Miss Rutherford?"

"I live in Myrtle Beach, South Carolina and have a Private Investigation office. My master's degree is in Criminal Justice and I was training for an attorney because my father had his heart set on it. I didn't care for the work and was lucky to get a job on the local police force, but after a serious injury on the job, I decided to open my own office. I have a wonderful staff of two. However, we've so much business I'll have to hire more qualified operatives."

"How interesting. I bet you could write a book about some of your cases. Oh, here's Jim now. Hello, Jim. May I introduce you to Miss Hannah Rutherford from Myrtle Beach, South Carolina. She has business that requires your presence. Miss Rutherford, this is Mr. Bridges. I'm sure you'll find him competent and helpful."

Hannah and Jim shook hands and exchanged pleasantries. Jim got a cup of coffee and sat down by Hannah.

"Now, how may I help you? What brings you this way?"

Hannah gave him the letter from the firm of Perkins, Greer and Hawkins to read. "Mr. Perkins, the senior of the firm, ask me to give this to whomever I worked with here." She waited to give him a few minutes to read the letter stating that she represented their firm and they would appreciate his cooperation.

"Yes, Miss Rutherford. How do you need my help?"

"I'm authorized to give you the bare essentials. The law firm, for whom I'm working, is representing a woman in a divorce case. She was badly abused and kept from having any money to save or spend for herself. Her husband is a high-ranking military officer with a prominent family name. She is sure she has heard him speak of owning property here in Florida and knows he plans to retire here some day. She is hoping that she can find the information of the property he owns because he purchased it after they were married and while she was still working and contributing to the family income. He insisted that she stop working and stay home just to wait on him. Is it possible to get any information about such property? If so, she might be legally able to demand a substantial amount for her own upkeep. She is only in her late forties and has been married twenty-five years. She is afraid she can't find a job and have an income and needs the reassurance of having something to count on."

Ginny was upset hearing this. "If she's telling the truth she certainly deserves some compensation. Jim, can you search the records for the information?"

"I sure can. There's nothing I'd like better. Most police are excellent about protecting and serving, but once in a while there's a bad apple. This sounds like a real rotten one. Let's go up to the records office and get to work."

Hannah was relieved. "I'm so happy that we can at least make an effort. I was afraid there was nothing we could do. Thank you, Ginny. I'm glad I met you."

"It's all my pleasure. Good luck." Ginny bustled out to her office and left Jim and Hannah to go about their business.

Three hours later Hannah rubbed her aching back and stood to stretch.

"Gracious. His family sure owns a lot of property. I hope we can separate his from the family."

Jim chuckled. "Take heart. Knowing his name helps tremendously. He does own property jointly with his brother and some woman. I need to find who she is. Barry," he called to a man passing through the room, "come here, please."

Jim was not a tall man; maybe an inch taller than Hannah. He was wiry and muscled with lots of energy. His brown hair was cut in such a way that Hannah suspected he had been in the military. She guessed him to be early to middle thirties. His hazel eyes showed laughter and intelligence. She didn't dare smile or laugh aloud because Barry topped both of them by a foot.

Barry was a handsome African American, no more than thirty, well over six feet, with lively brown eyes and the sweetest smile. He waited patiently for Jim to tell him what he wanted.

Jim introduced Barry and Hannah telling her that Barry was the best detective they had. "Barry, we need help in determining who a woman is and what relationship she has to this man. Can you do that for me?"

"I sure can. In fact, I can tell you right now who she is. She works in the law office where my mother works. She married a police officer about seven years ago who just disappeared. We did find him in the military and then back on the east coast."

"Did she ever get a divorce?" Hannah asked anxiously.

"I don't think so. She kept hoping that something had happened to his memory in the military and he would show up any day. Why? What's going on?"

Hannah drew herself up to her full height which still kept her much shorter than Barry. 'What's going on is that when he married this woman, he was already married to another woman where I live and work. Are you positive about this information?"

"I sure am. Would you like to talk to her?"

"Yes, but may I first call the attorney for whom I'm getting this information and ask him what he wants me to do?"

She thanked Barry and asked him if he would be around. He assured her that he would be here for a few hours. Jim took her to his office and told her to sit at the desk in his chair and be comfortable. "I'm going to step out and give you some privacy. If you need anything, or want me to return, pick up the phone and dial 2 3." He left closing the door behind him.

Hannah dialed the private phone of Attorney Perkins. "Hello?"

"Mr Perkins?"

"Yes, who is this?"

"I'm sorry. This is Hannah Rutherford. I've just found some startling news that I need to discuss with you before I act upon it."

"All right. Shoot."

She proceeded to tell him all she had discovered. "Do you want me to talk to this woman and get her input?"

"Heavens above. Good and bad news. It's good to know my client will be better off than she thought, but in the meantime, an innocent woman is going to be drug into this and hurt."

"I thought of that. Do you want me to talk to her, and if so, how much should I tell her?"

"I trust you, Hannah. You've had excellent home training as well as job training. Tell her everything, but first ask her if she wants an attorney present. We don't want to be sued or to have unnecessary problems."

"I understand. My heart aches for both women. He's a real slime ball and doesn't deserve to be a military officer, nor does he deserve a good wife. Okay. I'll do my best with a lot of prayer. Be praying on your end, also."

"I will, darling girl. Just make sure you're not placing yourself in a dangerous situation. I suggest that you take the attorney and the detective with you for your protection. Oh, I don't mean physical protection, but if this ends up in court you don't want to be floundering alone."

Hannah dialed 2 3 and waited. Jim was soon back in his office. Hannah got up to give him his chair and walked around the desk to be seated in a visitor's chair.

"Well?" Jim was curious.

"Attorney Perkins asked me to go ahead and talk to the woman, but he also suggested that I take you and Barry with me. I hope you'll be willing and able to go. Do you think Barry will go with us?"

"I shall be glad to go with you. At this point I need to know the remainder of the story and the outcome. Let me ask Barry." He called a number and asked the secretary to call Barry to the phone.

Barry had to juggle some appointments, but felt he could go because he was acquainted with the woman personally. Barry said he would ask his mother to be with the woman when they talked to her because they are friends.

Barry called his mother and explained the situation to her. She of course wanted to be with her friend.

"I'm shocked to hear this, son. I met the man once and thought he was off in the military this whole time. Anna Marie did , too. She'll be devastated, but she needs to know. She'll not only be hurt, but she'll be embarrassed to be the second wife. but how could she know? Where do you want to met and when? She's like a daughter to me."

Barry turned to Hannah. "Where and when do you want to meet?"

Hannah looked at Jim. "Don't you gentlemen think it would be better tomorrow morning rather than sending her to bed with such heartbreaking news?"

Jim and Barry looked at each other and nodded. "You're a wise and compassionate woman, Hannah. She goes by the name of Mrs. Anna Marie Gable. Her maiden name was Falls. She'll want to take it back as quickly as possible." Barry looked uncomfortable.

Barry turned to the phone. "Mom, can you be at Anna Marie's house tomorrow morning at" he turned to look at Hannah and Jim.

"Ten," Jim suggested, and Hannah nodded.

"Mom, we'll meet you there at ten. Tell her we're coming and prepare her as much as you can without telling her the whole story or scaring her to death."

Barry talked to his mother a few more minutes, thanked her and said, "I love you, Mom", and then hung up.

Jim offered to take Hannah to dinner, but she politely refused. "I need to prepare for the meeting and I will feel like a dirty dog to tell her such awful news."

The three of them shook hands as Hannah thanked them for their help. Each went their own way after Jim offered to pick Hannah up at the motel the next morning.

Hannah was so sorry for the young woman, whom she'd never met, that her feet felt like lead dragging her as she walked slowly back to La Quinta.

After a light supper she sat out on a small patio and breathed the clean, crisp air. She closed her eyes and prayed silently for guidance tomorrow.

Opening her eyes she gasped at the wonder of the sky. It looked as if an artist had slung a palate and threw a kaleidoscope of beautiful colors across the western sky. *I've never seen such beauty.* She enjoyed it until it got too dark, and cooled off. She went in, took a shower, put on night clothes, and called Herb's cell phone.

"Hey, buddy, you should have seen the gorgeous sunset that I just saw. You sound down. What's going on there?"

"Brian is ready to either commit suicide or murder. He's so upset. I can't make him understand that he has all the evidence on his side. Thomas Chandler and his dirty attorney are saying that Brian killed his own wife and planned the whole thing. Thankfully we have Allen's testimony, the hatchet with Chandler's fingerprints and the tapes from the phone calls."

"Doesn't he understand this is par for the course? Of course Chandler's attorney is working for him and urging him to plead innocent." Hannah exclaimed

"Allen and I both have tried to explain to him. By the way, he finally let me call his minister. I told him the whole story and so did Allen. He prayed with Brian and told him to listen to us. When the Sturgills called, Brian broke down and cried telling them all that had gone on. Now they're upset and want to come down to testify for him. I had to convince them that it was even more important now for them to keep the children safe. No telling what Chandler would hire someone to do to them."

"I shiver thinking about it, Herb. I'll be through here in a couple of days and can come on back to help, but I still have cases to work on. Herb, we need more workers. Keep your ears and eyes open. We need qualified people with personalities that will work with us."

"Finish what you have to do, Hannah and get home safely. We miss you, but the work does take us on crazy journeys sometimes."

They talked a few more minutes and hung up. Hannah tossed and turned thinking of Brian's problems, the meeting tomorrow morning and all her cases. *Okay, this is the life you wanted so grin and bear it.*

Chapter Fifteen

Hannah dragged herself out of bed wondering why she felt so down, then she remembered the meeting with the second wife. Seven o'clock. She showered, dressed carefully in a light blue suit with a pink blouse and dark blue heels. Her hair took longer than usual because she couldn't decide whether to leave it down or put it up in a French twist. Finally leaving it down, she applied mascara, a light dusting of powder and coral lip gloss.

Ambling across to the lobby she was surprised to see Jim sitting there. He jumped up when he saw her.

"Good morning. I hope I'm not presuming too much, but I was hoping to take you out for breakfast."

"That's kind of you, but why don't you join me here and we can talk. I do have to go back to my room and get my briefcase."

"Won't they mind me staying? I don't live here."

"If anything is said, I'll put it on my expense account."

They each took Raisin Bran and two percent milk; a plate of slices of fruit and decaf. Jim also took a bagel and cream cheese.

They discussed how they would present the horrible news to Anna Marie in such a manner that it would not cause her any additional grief. Hannah went back to her room, gave another quick brush to her teeth, picked up her briefcase and joined Jim in the lobby.

"Have you been here previous to this visit, Hannah?"

"No. This is my first time in Florida. What I've seen so far is delightful. I'm just sorry I can't spend more time sightseeing. I'd love to go to Kissimmee and Orlando and all the other places where the wonderful attractions are. Have you been to our section of South Carolina?"

"Just driving through. Maybe I'll come up some time and visit you. What kind of cases do you handle?"

"All kinds, although we have the option of not accepting a case if it appears to be dangerous or untrue."

"What do you mean, untrue?"

"Well, if someone wanted to get another person in trouble and ask us to find evidence against them, and we felt it was just a case of a clash of personalities, we'd say we're too busy, or even tell them it doesn't sound true. I do not approve of spying on a spouse to aid in a divorce. If I can find evidence, such as I've found here, then I'll do that, but I refuse to be sleazy."

Jim laughed. "I know what you mean. I don't approve of spying, as you call it, either."

"Jim, I like Tallahassee as much as I've seen. Do you know any of the history?"

"I sure do. My dad was a history buff and researched everything you can imagine. I do know that the Apalachee Indians lived here as long ago as ten thousand B.C."

"Wow! I learned the Sewee Indians were where I now am, and that it was first established as a settlement on July 6, 1680. We're no where near that old; at least we have no record of it yet. I'm sorry. Please go on."

"Well it's established that they lived there in peace through the 1600s and were farmers. They also developed great pottery which sold as far north as the Great Lakes are now. We know that in 1539 Herendo de Soto came through here. The Spanish explorer, Narvaez, celebrated the first Christmas here. The poor Indians were almost wiped out by the diseases the settlers brought. When the remaining Indians moved out they named this Tallahassee, which means abandoned. The few Indians who stayed accepted the Christian faith. Twenty missions were built. Both the Spanish and the few Indians fled for their lives in the early 1700s when Colonel James Monroe of South Carolina, leading a big band of Creek Indians, attacked. In the late 1700s General Andrew Jackson became governor and chased them out. In 1821 the Territory of Florida was established, but this area quickly became know as lawless with gun fights and knife duels. A group called the Tallahassee Police Department was formed to promote law and order."

"My goodness, I'm impressed. I don't know that much about our history, but I'll correct that when I go back. Tell me more, please."

"Okay. Indian attacks, yellow fever, hurricanes and a big city fire of all wooden buildings almost destroyed the area. By 1845 Tallahassee was declared the capital of Florida. In the late 1800s wealthy Northerners bought a lot of property and opened hunting retreats. Plantation owners objected and there were a lot of hard feelings. In 1920 Tall Timber Research Station moved in to study ecological issues. In 1929 Dale Mabry Air Field opened and commercial aviation began. In 1960 the dogwood tree was voted the symbol of Tallahassee, and an annual parade was celebrated. By 1960 the schools were integrated, and in 1999 Tallahassee was recognized as an All America City. Hey. I could go on forever, but we're here now."

"Oh, I wish we could just ride around and sightsee, but this is my job. Believe me, I truly hate to do this."

Jim came around to open the door for Hannah. "I see Barry's car, so that means he's already inside. I hope he hasn't given anything away."

"I doubt that he has, Jim. He impressed me as being very professional."

Hannah turned to see a beautifully kept lawn, lots of flower beds, bird feeders hanging from trees and even butterfly bushes. The house was a pink brick with big picture windows in the living room and a good-sized window in what Hannah thought might be the kitchen. A tall flag pole proudly waving the American flag was in the front.

With her heart beating so hard Hannah thought Jim might hear it, they walked to the front door. Jim knocked, but before he completed the knock, the door was opened by Barry.

"Boy, am I glad to see you. She suspects that it's not good news, but I couldn't tell her anything. She is afraid it might be that her husband is dead or missing."

Stepping inside, Hannah was pleased to see white marble flooring with black swirls. To the right, against a wall was a red cedar table with a gilt-framed mirror above it. The room to the right was a large dining room and beyond that was the kitchen. Hannah remembered a driveway going around the side of the building and assumed the garage was near the back.

Barry led them to the left on a thick, white carpet. "Hannah Rutherford, this is my mother, Mrs. Martha Gladstone." Hannah could tell by the pride in his voice that he dearly loved his mother. "And this is Mrs. Anna Marie Gable." He then introduced Jim to Anna Marie.

Hannah greeted both women properly and accepted a seat near Anna Marie.

"Mom, you've met Jim, haven't you?"

"Yes, son I have. Jim, how are you?"

"I'm fine, thank you ma'am. And you?"

"Oh, I'm fine, but, like Anna Marie, I'm anxious to hear what this is all about."

"Yes, do you have bad news about my husband?" Anna Marie asked anxiously.

"You're husband is alive and well. Let me tell you a little about why I'm here. First I want you to know that you're free to request that you can call an attorney of your choice, although Jim is an attorney. Neither of us want to say or do anything to hurt you."

Anna Marie looked anxiously at Martha. What do you think I should do?"

"I don't know all that this is about, but I would suggest you just listen today and then call an attorney if you wish to do so."

The younger woman chewed her bottom lip and thought a moment. "Okay. What is it you want to tell me?"

Hannah took a deep breath. "I want you to know that I hate this, but it is my job. I own an investigation agency in Myrtle Beach, South Carolina."

Here she held out her badge and identification for Anna Marie to see. The young woman took them and read carefully.

"All right, but what does that have to do with me?"

"Well, sometimes attorneys hire an investigator to search records for them in other areas where they don't have the time or experience. The firm of Perkins, Greer and Hawkins. Mr. Jason Perkins is the senior partner and contacted me for this assignment." She gave Anna Marie the letter from Mr. Perkins stating that she was working for them.

"One of their clients has been married to a military officer for twenty-five years. He has been physically, mentally and emotional abusive. Lately he has been beating her enough to be hospitalized. His family is quite wealthy and has a lot of influence. She has been afraid to oppose them, but now she wants a divorce and asked Mr. Perkins to determine if her husband has property, or bank accounts, in Tallahassee where his family is."

Anna Marie gasped. "My husband is military and his family lives here. Are you trying to say her husband is my husband?"

"I'm afraid so. I could hardly believe my eyes when I discovered that he not only has property and money here, but has taken on a second wife."

"Second wife!? Does that mean our marriage is not official?" She started crying so hard that both Martha and Barry went to comfort her.

After several minutes, she gained control and through her sobs asked, "What should I do now?"

Hannah leaned over to take her hand. "I would call an attorney now and get all the information you can before you let him know you're aware of the situation. Of course, you realize that the first wife is entitled to half of his property and money, but I honestly don't know where you stand. That's why you need an attorney you can trust."

"There's one I trust that also attends the same church I do. Would you stay and tell him all of this?"

Hannah hesitated. "Oh, dear. I was hoping to head home, but I'm sure Mr. Perkins will not object to me staying one more day to talk to your attorney. When can you contact him?"

"Right now." She jumped up and ran toward the kitchen.

"There's a phone right there," Hannah pointed out to the others.

"Dear, she needs privacy," Martha explained.

"Of course."

In a few minutes she was back stating, Arnold said he could be here in twenty minutes if you're willing to wait. I'll even fix lunch for us."

"Honey, you don't have to feed us," Hannah protested.

"Arnold was on his way to lunch. I bribed him to come now and I'd feed him. We need to eat."

Hannah looked quizzically at Anna Marie, "You seem to be taking this a little easier. I was afraid you would be so devastated that I would feel guilty for putting you in the hospital," she smiled.

"After the initial shock, and talking to Arnold, I settled down. To tell you the truth, I haven't been happy about this marriage. We met at a church social when he attended once with his mother. We dated just a short time and were married four years ago. He was wonderful at first and then had to report back to the military. When he came for a quick visit he was abrasive, quick to find fault and very unhappy. I did not know that he was feeling pressured because of bigamy. I don't hear from him often and he isn't romantic at all. I meant to ask him, when he contacted me again, if he was unhappy in our marriage. Drat, there's the phone. Excuse me."

"Hello. Mike!" She turned to look at them and held out a hand as if to say, what do I do? They all shook their heads.

"When can you come home?" She listened for a few minutes. "Yes, I'll be happy to take care of it. I love you." She hung up and shook her head.

"He never says I love you or acts as if he hears me. He wants me to get an important piece of mail that will be coming to his parents' home and not open it, but leave it with our attorney, who happens to be Arnold Jenkins," she chortled.

Barry rushed to answer the knock at the door. A man of about sixty with white hair and wise blue eyes stood there. He, too, had to look up at Barry as he was only about five-nine. He had a medium build, but very good condition which showed either that he worked out in a gym or exercised on his own. As he smiled and came through the door he shook hands with Barry.

Hannah approved of his very professional grey suit, white shirt and grey and black tie with polished black shoes.

Barry escorted him in and Anna Marie introduced every one. "Let's eat first and then get down to business. Arnold has to get back to his office and I don't want to keep him too long." She invited then into the dining room and seated them around a beautiful oval oak table with matching well-padded chairs. A six drawer, three on each side, furniture stood opposite an oak china cabinet with beautiful dishes and glasses. When asked about the furniture Anna Marie explained that her parents had given her this set where they bought it freshly made in North Carolina at a factory. The drawers held napkin, table cloths, candles, silver ware and needed accessories for dining.

"I hope none of you are allergic to chicken." They laughed. "I have chicken salad sandwiches on rye or whole wheat bread, or if you don't want a sandwich just eat it as a salad. There are deviled eggs, pickled beats, raw celery, carrots and cauliflower. Help yourselves. You have a choice between coffee, milk, lemonade or water." Two chose coffee, all the rest wanted lemonade.

After a delicious, filling lunch, they all thanked her and Hannah offered to help her clean up.

"No, but thank you. I'll put the food that's left in the refrigerator and join you in the living room. Hannah, if you don't mind, show Arnold your credentials and explain to him what all of this is about."

"If that's what you want I shall be delighted to start."

As they were seated in the living room, Arnold turned to Jim. "You're an attorney. Why did she call me, or is it something that you're bringing against her.?"

"No. I'm certainly not against Anna Marie. My heart goes out to her. Hannah will explain who she is and she needed my expertise in property law in the state of Florida.

I'm along to help her and because I want to see justice done."

Arnold looked hard at all of them, grunted and turned to Hannah. "All right, young lady, what do you have to tell me?"

"Nothing good, sir. First here are my credentials and the letter from the attorney for whom I'm working." He took them, carefully read all of them, nodded and handed it back to Hannah. She carefully told him the entire story.

Hannah finished with, "This is one of the difficult jobs because I get so caught up in other peoples troubles that it actually hurts. I do think that Anna Marie needs to discuss this with you and allow you to advise her as to steps she needs to take. I do strongly feel that she does not need to let him know that she knows all of this until she is ready to do whatever the two of you have decided."

"I sure agree with you on that." He turned to Anna Marie who had slipped in and was sitting on a piano bench near him. "Honey, we'll go over this with a fine tooth comb, so to speak, and then decide how we'll handle it. Are you aware that you're not legally married in the state of Florida?"

"Yes, that occurred to me. Something else. I wanted a baby so badly and he would never agree saying wait until he retired. Now I'm so thankful that an innocent little baby is not mixed up in this calamity."

Hannah stood. "Anna Marie, I'm sincerely glad to meet you, and truthfully so sorry that you've had this fall on you. With your attorney's help you can come out of this wonderfully well. I don't know what you can do, but I'd sure hold out for ownership of this house and all the furniture."

"I'm thinking ahead of you, young lady," Arnold laughed. "We'll get through this and remember I said we'll. I'll be with you all the way. Now do you want to tell your parents alone or do you want the two of us to talk to them?"

"Please go with me to tell them. My dad has such a temper he might decide to take a shotgun and go after Mike. Arnold, should I talk to his parents? They've been wonderful to me and I feel sad for them."

Hannah was shaking her head quickly. Arnold put his arm around Anna Marie's shoulder. "At this moment I don't want you saying a word to them. Wait until we decide how we'll handle it. I know you'll see them at church. When they find out later, tell them I wouldn't allow you to talk about it."

Hannah shook hands with Arnold and thanked him for taking over. She then thanked Barry for his help and hugged Anna Marie and Martha. They left with Jim driving Hannah to her motel.

Jim parked and walked Hannah to the lobby of the motel. "I wish you'd have dinner with me."

"It sounds delightful and I do hope we'll meet again. I can't thank you enough, Jim, for all your help. If you have a charge for your services, or if Barry does, Mr. Perkins will be glad to pay."

"No. I don't want payment, but I am curious as to how Anna Marie and her attorney will handle this. Barry's mother, as you know, feels very close to Anna Marie, so, Barry won't want pay. Please say you'll keep in touch. I'd love to see you again."

"I'd like to see you, too. Thank you for the dinner invitation, but I'm going to try to get as far as Augusta tonight and then go on home tomorrow."

Jim leaned over to kiss her on the cheek. "Get home safely and call me so that I'll know you're safe. I know you have cases waiting for you."

"Thank you, again," she turned to leave and wheeled around. "Jim, I could sure use a good attorney on my team if you decide to come up my way."

"One never knows, does one, he answered with a chuckle."

CHAPTER SIXTEEN

Taking one last stroll around town, Hannah enjoyed the cool evening breeze. Wearing slacks, a long-sleeved blouse and a sweater was all she needed.

At the end of a block she turned to go back to the motel sure that she could sleep now. A man passed so close that he almost brushed her shoulder.

"Sorry," he muttered as he walked on.

Hannah took a quick look and whirled around. "Sir. Sir. Wait, please."

He stopped and turned.

"It is you!" she gasped. "I couldn't believe my eyes. What are you doing down here? How are you?"

He looked confused. "I'm sorry, do I know you?"

"Oh, I'm so sorry. I am just so surprised and thrilled to see you that I forgot. I'm Hannah Rutherford. I'm the one who found you and paid your hospital bills after you were attacked near the courthouse."

"Sure. Now I remember. I wanted to talk to you but Chief Wingate took me out in an ambulance one night and brought me here. I was working for him and the sheriff and had to follow their wishes."

"You were working for both of them. I don't understand."

"Didn't I hear you're a private investigator?"

"Yes, I am. I have an agency on Oak Street not far from the courthouse."

"We need to talk. Do you have time to get a cup of coffee and chat?"

"I'm at the La Quinta and they have coffee in the lobby all of the time. Why don't we go back there and sit in comfort in the lobby. It's big enough until we won't be overheard."

He hesitated. "Okay, although I feel awkward taking coffee from your place and not paying for it."

"You can offer to pay, but they'll tell you it's all right."

"Let's go then."

They walked quickly back to the motel. The manager graciously told him he could have the coffee as he was with a paying guest.

"To begin, my name is Richard Longbow, and yes, I'm part Native American. That's Lieutenant Longbow. I was first on the city force and then as a deputy sheriff. I finally made detective and was so proud of myself. I was drafted (he laughed) to go undercover and try to determine who, in the courthouse, could be connected with drug running. I guess I wasn't as undercover as I thought."

He paused to take a sip of coffee. Hannah could see from the expression in his eyes that this was hard on him.

"I'm only telling you this, Hannah, because both the Chief and the Sheriff highly recommended you. I had intended to ask for your help, but I was found out and beat up before I could ask you. Much to my surprise, you were the one who found me."

"Were you successful in discovering the criminals?"

"Yes and no. Let me explain."

"Please continue."

"I did find the ones that were evidently involved, but I had no definite proof to take to court."

"Can you tell me who they are?"

"Sorry. It's an ongoing investigation and I'm not at liberty to divulge that information. The Chief might share with you, but I doubt it at this time."

"All right. I certainly understand. Are you returning to Myrtle Beach soon?"

"I can't, but as soon as I can, I'll look you up. It's been a year now and I hope they've forgotten what I look like."

"If you hesitate to go back to work for the city or county, I sure can use you."

"Thank you. I'll keep that in mind. I might even surprise you."

"This is lovely, but if you'll please forgive me, I have to get up early and drive back home. I meant to leave tonight and go part of the way, but I was fortunate to find you. I've thought of you and worried about you all this time."

"I'll see that you're reimbursed for the money you spent on me."

"Forget it. It was a pleasure and a blessing to me to be able to help."

"Righto. Good night, dear lady. Safe trip home. Give me your address and phone so that I can keep in touch."

* * * * *

Hannah thankfully pulled in to her own garage a little after ten on Saturday night. She felt as if she had been gone forever. She brought everything out of the car and into the house. Placing dirty clothes in the washer, she started it and placed her notes for the case on the desk so she could type them for Mr. Perkins and keep a copy for herself.

Taking a long, wonderful shower and then dressing for bed she called Herb to tell him she was home and that they'd have a long talk after church tomorrow.

"I'm so beat, and have so many thoughts running through my poor brain, that I'm not sure who I am. There is a lot of great and interesting news to share. How is Brian and what is going on?"

"Brian is still a nervous wreck. I've had to almost hog tie him to keep him from running up to see his babies. Even though Chandler is in jail, that doesn't mean he hasn't hired someone to cause trouble. We've learned that it will take at least sixty days for the psychiatrists to do a good job, so we're still in limbo. I have other cases that I've tried to work, but I really need to come to the office on a regular basis."

"Mark Phluger is on sick leave after being shot on duty. He isn't allowed to work, but I know it's driving him crazy. Maybe he'd be willing to stay with Brian some. Think about it and talk to Brian," Hannah offered.

"Okay. See you tomorrow. Good night. Rest well."

"Thank you. You, too."

She then called Victoria and had to forcefully end the call because Victoria was so thrilled she was home.

Even though it was late, she thought carefully and called Jim Bridges. He, too, would have talked too long if she had not pleaded tiredness and sleepiness. He was ecstatic to hear from her.

Her last call was to Richard Longbow which was short.

Literally falling in bed, she quickly went to sleep and didn't stir until the alarm rang at six thirty. Dressing, she went for her much needed run which she had missed. She returned, showered, dressed, ate a quick breakfast, picked up her Bible and hurried to church.

After church, she drug home and collapsed on a lounge chair to read the morning paper and drink a Diet Coke.

As she started to fix something for lunch, her doorbell rang. Herb stood there with a grin as wide as his shoulders. He grabbed her up and hugged her, carrying her into the living room and depositing her in her chair.

Laughing, she swatted a him. "You nuthead. What do you think you're doing?"

"I'm hoping to kidnap you and take you out to lunch. How about going down near the landing for a good seafood meal?"

"Sounds great. I'm hungry and I won't have to dress up. Let me get some shoes on and I'll race you to the car."

She laughed when she came out to see Herb already in the car ready to drive. They went to the Surf and Turf on the waterfront and had a luscious meal and a delightful conversation. Hannah brought Herb up-to-date about the case she fell into in Tallahassee about the bigamist husband. She then told him of finding the mysterious man with amnesia.

Herb was very interested in both news and hoped she'd be able to hear the results of the case that Mr. Perkins had asked her to cover.

"I'm anxious to hear, also. I'd like to know how it is settled. Have you had any more incidences of stolen body parts?"

Herb looked angry. "Yes, they're getting bolder since they've never been caught. I feel so sorry for the families that have to take a loved one and have a funeral, or a memorial and there's still no closure."

"I know what you mean. I do, too. Herb, this was delicious, but I need to walk a little and maybe get more comfortable. As usual I made a pig of myself and I feel stuffed."

"Good. I love to walk along the waterfront. Let me pay and we'll leave."

They started walking south from the restaurant. After about ten minutes they saw a crowd in front of them and police cars. Coming closer they were able to hear the comments from the people gathered around.

"Pardon me," Hannah said to a woman, "what's going on? Is someone hurt?"

"Hurt! For the love of God, woman, an innocent young girl has been killed and her body parts are cut out of her."

Hannah grabbed Herb's hand and pushed through the crowd to where two policemen stood. She recognized Sgt. Alex Burke with whom she had worked. She didn't know the rookie that was training with him.

"Alex. What in the world?"

"Hannah, how glad I am to see you. This crowd is getting unruly. They seem to think I should conjure up the murderer out of thin air, and they're scared spitless. I can't blame them, but we can't seem to break them up. Backup is slow responding because of a tragic accident on the highway and an arson fire with two bodies in the house."

Hannah introduced Herb to them. "Alex, I'm not on the force any more, but we can help. Why don't we interview witnesses until you get some help. You need to get statements while it's clear in their minds."

"I'll probably get called down for it, but go ahead."

Herb insisted on staying with Hannah. They listened to a few people, some all trying to talk at once in the excitement. Finally one woman, with a yapping little poodle, grabbed Hannah's arm. Hannah could tell she was frightened by her wide eyes and wavering voice.

"I saw something that didn't seem right to me."

Hannah held the woman's hand while Herb took notes.

"Mrs.?--"

"Fletcher. Mrs. Harrison Fletcher. But call me Irene."

"Fine, Irene. What did you see? Take a deep breath, calm down and tell me."

"I heard a scream and Sweetie Pie started barking. When I ran to my window, I didn't see that poor, unfortunate girl laying there, but I did see two young people hurry off carrying those Styrofoam Igloo containers. I know what they are because we have one. They seemed to be heavy as if they were full of ice and something heavy."

"Can you describe the people that were leaving with the containers?"

"The boy was just average. He was blonde, medium and dressed all in white-- white slacks, white top, white tennis shoes, and ----- the girl was in a white dress with a white sweater and white tennis shoes. They didn't look back, so I didn't see their faces. She was slender and a little bit shorter than the boy. I would say maybe late twenties."

"What color was her hair?" Herb asked.

"Dark, I think. She had something like a white net over her head. I was too far away to see much, but after the police came, I thought it was strange that they hurried away from where the girl was laying."

Herb and Hannah looked at each other and both said, "Medical. Or maybe they're trying to throw the police off by making them think it's medical students."

Hannah walked to Alex. He had to stay near the body because the curious crowd was getting too close and the rookie had his hands full keeping order.

"Hannah, we're both in for a tongue lashing. Chief Wingate himself is on his way." Alex worried.

"Well, we have something that will delight him. I bet it's the first break in the case." She told him what the woman had said. By then the Chief joined them.

"Hannah, and Herb, what in the blue blazes are you doing here? You shouldn't even have your nose in this. What did I tell you?"

Alex finally calmed him down enough to ask him to read Hannah's notes. They didn't want to talk about it where people in the crowd could hear.

"Who is this?", the Chief roared. "I want to talk to her?"

Hannah took him over to the woman's house nearby while Herb stayed to help Alex with crowd control. Herb looked around disgusted. "Where are all these people when we really need them, and where did they come from? There must be a hundred in this crowd. Vultures."

Rookie James McDonald explained. "A few live here the year around, but most of these cottages along the waterfront are rented to snowbirds."

Herb continued to ask people milling around if they had seen or heard anything. None had only heard the scream that the girl had given who discovered the body.

"Where is she? Is she still in the crowd?"

"No," one man told Herb. "Her boyfriend hurried her away. They went toward the shops down on the waterfront."

"Would you recognize her if you saw her again?" Herb asked.

"I think so. She was wearing a pink swim suit with a white lace cover-up and flip-flops."

"Please stay here with me. I need to wait until someone comes to help this officer and then we'll walk down there and see if you can find her."

In less than five minutes a patrol car pulled up and two officers got out.

"Hey, Jimmy," one called. "What's going on?"

"Boy, am I glad to see you. I'm left here in charge of crowd control and this nice detective is the only one that has helped me. We have our hands full. The crowd gets bigger by the minute."

"That's what we're here for, to help." He stopped in front of Herb almost as tall as Herb.

"You're a detective? A detective where?"

"At one time I was on the city force. Now I'm in a private office with Hannah Rutherford. I'm sure you've heard of the Lost Cause Detective Agency."

"I sure have and I have heard a lot of good about Hannah. So you're working there now. Why are you working here today?"

"Sorry, I didn't get your name." Herb spoke firmly.

"Oh yes. I'm Lieutenant Jason McCormack."

They shook hands and Herb continued talking.

"There was a murder and a lot of people gathered around. The patrolman had no help and I volunteered to help. Now I'm going down to the stores with this kind gentleman and find the girl that discovered the murderer working, screamed and ran."

"This man can identify the girl?"

"My name is Ralph Borden and yes, I can identify the girl. If we don't get down there she could disappear."

"Let's go," Herb turned to hurry away.

"Hey, hey! Where do you think you're going? You can't go messing into police business. You're not authorized." Jason angrily stated.

"Any citizen can provide any information to a police investigation. No, I'm no longer on the city force, but this man can identify someone very important to this case. If we don't get down there, she may be gone and the police will lose valuable information. You can't go because you have to stay here and help with crowd control. I'm **sure** not authorized for that. Come on, Ralph." Herb hurried away with Jason sputtering and Ralph looking frightened and unsure.

Sure enough, as they got within a few feet of the "tourist stores" and snack bar, Ralph called out excitedly, "There she goes. She and that fellow are going up to where the cars are parked."

Herb started running calling, "Miss. Miss. Please wait a minute."

The young couple looked back and took off running to a red Toyota sports car. Just as they got almost to their car, a police car pulled up and Chief Wingate jumped out.

"Stop right there. You're not in trouble, but you will be if you run."

The couple did stop looking anxious and frightened. "Why us?" the young man stuttered. "We haven't done anything."

"No one said you did," the Chief answered them. "I think these two men have a few questions for you."

Herb took Ralph's arm and pulled him closer. "Take a close look. Is this the lady you saw?"

"Yes, it is, and I'll swear to that."

The girl burst out crying and the young man was angry. He hugged her close to him. "She didn't commit any crime. Why don't you let her alone?"

"Ma'am", the Chief began, "did you see a crime being committed? Weren't you close to the woman that was killed up there on the boardwalk?"

She nodded, unable to talk for crying.

"So what?" The young man was still very angry. "She didn't commit any crime."

"We need a description of the person or persons who did commit the crime. If we don't get a lead on them now, you might be the next one lying just as that poor girl is."

"Can we talk privately?" the young man asked.

"Sure. Get in here." The Chief opened his back door and motioned for them to get in and sit. He closed the door and stepped aside to talk to Herb and to meet Ralph.

"Herb, I was first annoyed with you, but when Pvt. McDonald told me how you helped with crowd control until the Lt. got there, I realized why you were helping. Too, Hannah ripped me up and down for not backing you." He laughed.

He turned to Ralph. "Thank you for being a good citizen. I'm Chief Wingate."

"Yes, I know who you are. I'm Ralph Borden. I'm a coach at the local high school and try to instill in my students that they must respect and cooperate with our police."

"Thank God for teachers who do more than stand in a classroom and draw a paycheck. Did you see anything?"

"Not really. I was getting out of my car and heard a scream. When I looked up, this couple was running toward me and passed me. When I looked back to see what they were running from, I saw the body."

"This was the couple you saw?"

"Yes, sir."

They heard the man knocking on the window of the car. The handles are removed from the back seats in a police car and there's a steel mesh between the people in the back and the police in the front. This keeps the prisoners from escaping or doing harm to the police.

The Chief hurried over and opened the door. "Are you ready to tell us now what you saw? We can talk here or go down to the station."

"We'll talk," the woman sniffed.

Chief Wingate took a notebook from his pocket and a pen. "First I need your names, address and telephone."

"I'm Anna Marie Wingate," the girl giggled. "No relation, I don't think. I live at 826 N. Ocean Blvd. phone 555-8743. Is that what you need?"

"For the present. Thank you. And you, sir."

"I'm Andrew Mason, 486 N. Ocean Blvd., phone 555-9764."

"Thank you both. Now tell me what you saw."

They looked at each other and then Anna Marie spoke. "We were walking along just talking and I heard a sound like someone moaning or calling for help. I looked ahead of us and saw a couple bending over someone on the boardwalk. I thought the person was hurt and they were helping whoever it was. We just walked on until they looked up and saw us coming."

Andrew took up the account. "I saw two people in white uniforms bending over someone on the walk. They saw us and ran. That surprised me that they would run so I called out, 'hey, what's going on?' they just ran faster. I did see that they were each carrying an igloo that looked as if it might be full of ice or something. That's all we saw until we got close and saw it was the body of a young woman and she was bloody. Anna Marie screamed and people started running toward us. She ran from me down the walk and I took off after her. I didn't know why she would run."

"I just hated to look at all that blood and didn't know what had happened. Why would they run instead of helping her?"

Andrew continued. "I did notice something peculiar. The smaller person, whom I assumed to be a nurse, ran strangely. I had a feeling it might be a man wearing a wig and dress."

"Why did you assume she was a nurse?" Hannah asked. Chief Wingate glared at her.

"They were both in white clothes and white shoes. The smaller person even had on white stockings. They could have been interns, or someone dressed as such trying to leave false clues."

Chief Wingate smiled at them. "Thank you. This is more information than we've received so far and it is most helpful. Come to the station as soon as you can and give us a statement that can be used in our files."

"Do we have to?" the girl whined.

"Yes. You do. A good citizen would be glad to do so."

The couple left and the Chief turned to Hannah. "I've tried to keep you out of this, but you keep turning up like a bad penny." He smiled and hugged her. He reached to shake Herb's hand and thank him for his help.

"We do have a little more information, but the more we get the more puzzling the crime gets. It's clear body parts are being harvested, but by whom, and who are they selling to?"

Herb left stating he wanted to know what was happening to Thomas Chandler. Hannah left to go back to the office.

Chief Wingate got in his car with a heavy heart . *A lot of little clues, but none good enough to catch these vile people. The mayor is on my neck because the crime has not been close to be solved. I can't work magic.* He huffed and pulled away.

CHAPTER SEVENTEEN

Three days later Hannah was alone in the office. She was thinking of the cases on which they were working and of the ones that were difficult to solve. As she got up to get a cup of coffee she heard a noise as someone came in the front door.

What have I been thinking of? I'm alone and back here where no one can see me from the street. I've gotten warnings over the phone and attempts on my life. I can't sit back here and be a victim. She quickly walked to the doorway of the room. "Is someone there?"

"Oh, thank God," a man's voice answered as a man came running back to her. "Please, you have to save my life. I don't know where to turn or what to do."

"Please, come in and sit down. I shall be glad to listen to you and do whatever I can. Would you like a coffee or something else to drink?"

"No. I don't want anything to eat or drink. I just want help."

"As I said, I'll do what I can. What is the problem?"

"My name is Alexander Falls. I'm married, but no children yet although I'd love to have some. I work at Isaac's Jewelry Store and often travel for them to appraise jewelry or gems from other areas. I have been on a trip and wasn't supposed to come home until tomorrow. I came home a day early and was eager to see my wife. I brought her some jewelry and was anxious to give it to her." He paused. Hannah waited patiently.

"I eased in the front door expecting to surprise her. The phone rang just as I passed it, but before I could pick it up I heard her answer and squeal out, 'hello lover'. I gently picked up the phone near me and quietly listened. She reminded the man that I was not at home but would return tomorrow. He then said, ' I have a man for the job but he wants twenty thousand dollars to get rid of him for you'. My name was not mentioned but I did understand that my wife and this man were planning to have me killed. I didn't know what to do, so I quietly eased back out and ran. I saw your sign and knew I could get help here."

"I will agree that it sounded suspiciously like they might be talking about you and -- er -- getting rid of you. I don't make it a habit to handle cases like this or divorce cases. I can give you the name of another agency that does do work of this nature. I really suggest that you talk to Chief Wingate and let him advise you."

"Go to the police! That's the help you'll give me?" He jumped up so quickly that his chair tilted over backward. He was too rattled to notice as he paced back and forth.

"First, I don't have a big enough staff to cover what you need to have done, and we are swamped with cases now. Please let me contact Chief Wingate for you."

"And let you charge me a big amount for doing nothing."

"There is no charge. I don't charge for doing nothing, and I often don't charge in rare cases. I used to be on the force, so I know Chief Wingate will be glad to listen and help you."

"Well," he reluctantly stated, "if you think that's the best way to go."

"It is. I'll make the call now."

It was fortunate that Chief Wingate was in his office and made time to run over. He listened courteously to the upset man."

"Mr. Falls, we don't know for sure that you're assumptions are correct. I would suggest that you contact the agency that Miss Rutherford suggested. They will place a listening device on your phone and have your wife followed. They'll make recordings and take pictures. When, and if, you get the proof that you think is there, then you can ask as attorney to follow up. I would not suggest that you discuss any of this with your wife at this time. Go on as you have been and say little. At this time I can't do anything. I can only say that I'm truly sorry that you're going through this. I can see you're very upset. I'll wish you the very best and my last advice is talk to God." He walked out.

Alex sat thoughtful for a few minutes. "I'm sorry I spoke so harshly to you. I'm just shocked and upset."

"I can imagine how you must feel. I wish I could help, but I've explained." Hannah explained.

"I know. Would you please write the name of that agency and I'll think about going to them."

"I'll be delighted to write it for you," she reached for a pad and pen. "I'll even call them if you want me to do so."

"Would you? Thank you. I can't believe how nice you've been and not able to take my case."

She smiled, picked up her phone and dialed the Discrete and Fulfilling Agency. "Hi, Maisey. This is Hannah Rutherford. Is your boss in? I need to speak to him." She waited a few seconds. "Hello Jeff. I'm fine. How are you doing? Jeff, there's a man in my office desperately in need of your services. I'm unable to do what he needs. I'd like to send him to you and know he was getting the best of attention. Thank you so much. I'll be in touch."

She gave the paper with the name, address and phone number on it. "He'll see you personally immediately if you can get there. You can trust them. I just have one request."

"What's that?" He stood puzzled.

"Keep in touch and let me know what's going on. I hope to be able to do more in the future when I can hire additional detectives."

Relieved, he kept shaking her hand until she thought he wouldn't let go.

"I'll sure do that and I can't thank you enough. It has helped just to talk about it and know that someone cares." He hurried out.

Hannah rocked back in her chair with a smile. It always made her feel good if she knew someone was helped. She thought for a few minutes and picked up the phone. Before she could make the call, Herb breezed in full of excitement. She replaced the phone to listen to Herb. Victoria came in from going to the bank and running errands. The three of them gathered in Hannah's office.

"I'm just so hap-hap- happy, I could burst."

Victoria hit his shoulder. "Well, tell us before you burst and spoil the fun."

"I just heard that the psychologists have completed their tests on Thomas Chandler and have concluded that he is sane enough to stand trial. They do agree that he is a psychopath. He's still in jail and will be tried within the next month. What a way for Brian to start a new year."

"What a relief, and I know Brian will be thrilled. Does this mean he can now bring his children home?" Victoria asked.

"Oh, I wouldn't advise that yet," Hannah said. "Chandler could have hired someone to abduct the children to keep Brian from testifying. They're doing fine where they are and are in good hands. I knew Brian misses them, but it will be better to make sure the way will be completely clear before he brings them home."

"Okay gang. Back to a call I was going to make when you folks came in."

She told them of the man who needed surveillance and phone tapping. "We are not prepared to do that for a number of reasons. I don't like the idea and we don't have enough operators to take on such a job. I was just getting ready to call the two men in Florida I told you about and see if they would consider working with us. Is that okay with you two?"

"You're the boss," Herb exploded. "Why should you even ask us?"

"Out of courtesy. We do have to work together. I know you'll like these two men if they're willing to give us a try."

"Where would we put them?" Victoria asked anxiously.

"Well my dear, if they accept, you and I will have to go office hunting. In fact, it wouldn't be a bad idea to look anyway. We are expanding and need more room. How close are you, Victoria, in achieving your goal?"

"One more semester and I'll, hopefully, be where I want to be. One more piece of good news. The doctor says that I've made such great progress that he's taking the brace off my leg next week. I just need to be careful for a while to not strain my leg and back."

Hannah jumped up to hug Victoria, but Herb beat her to it. They cheered with her. "See, we'll need to have an office for you and hire someone to manage the desk and maybe another one to do bookkeeping and finances."

"You mean I've been doing all that all this time and you'll hire two people to do what I was doing?" She pretended to huff.

"We have been too small for two, but if we enlarge, we'll need them. I think I know a lady to be receptionist. We'll need a good, trustworthy bookkeeper."

"What woman do you have in mind? Herb asked.

"Remember Anna Mae Harkins that works at the police station?" He nodded. "She's getting ready to retire after twenty-six years there and I know she'll be bored out of her skull. She's only fifty-eight and too young to just sit down. I know we can trust her to keep confidences and she'll be great to work with."

Herb jumped up. "I'd give her a couple of weeks to relax and, yes, get bored and we'd love to have her, if she's willing." Victoria agreed.

Victoria started out and turned. "I met a young single mother who is taking Criminal Justice courses. She said she didn't have money to continue and is looking for work that she can fit around her four year old son. She has worked at an insurance company as bookkeeper. I don't know her well, but maybe she would be interested."

"Give me her name and I'll have Chief Wingate check her out before we offer her the job. Thank you both for all you've done. I couldn't have fulfilled my dreams without you."

"I'm getting out of here before I have to wade through it," Herb laughed. "I'm on my way to talk to Brian and then I have another case I need to check on, so I probably won't see you again today."

"Stay safe, my friend," Hannah called to him.

Victoria came back. "Hannah, I have favor to ask."

"Ask away."

"I have a class tonight and I need to get some groceries before I go home. My cupboards are looking like Old Mother Hubbard's."

Hannah laughed. "Go on. I'll close and go to the Down Home Realty office and see if they have larger office space."

"You own this building. Will you sell it or rent it?"

"I haven't decided yet. The three of us, or hopefully the five of us, will get together and discuss that. Go on home. Have a good night and sleep peacefully."

Hannah took care of some paper work and filing and then closed up. She decided to walk across the street and down a block to the real estate office.

As she crossed the street she looked carefully in both directions. Wonder of wonders -- no traffic. She was part of the way across the four lane street when she became aware of the sound of a car. She looked up in time to run and jump on the opposite sidewalk as the car picked up speed and headed straight toward her.

"I saw that." Eighty-eight year old Robert Hudson hobbled over and helped Hannah up where she had sprawled when she hit the sidewalk. "That dern fool looked like he headed right for you."

Alice Kramer ran out of the ladies' dress shop. "Hannah, are you hurt? I've already called the police."

"Oh, thank you both, but I've only hurt my pride." She laughed. "Remember what our mothers told us about wearing good underclothes in case we had an accident? That's what I thought of as I fell with my skirt hiking up."

By then Patrolman Ronald Jenkins pulled up. "What's going on here?"

Hannah, Alice and Mr. Hudson all started talking at once.

"Whoa. One at a time, please," he said as he got a notebook and pen out.

"Now, who's first? What about you? You look as if you're the one the accident happened to. You're bleeding on one knee and elbow."

"Well so I am," she chuckled. "I'll be sore tomorrow. I left my office over there and crossed over here. There was no traffic when I started to cross. About half way a car appeared out of nowhere and almost hit me. I made a leap in this direction and fell as I got to the sidewalk."

"I saw it. I saw it. The dern fool," Mr. Hudson stated excitedly. "This young lady was crossing, and, as she said, there was no traffic. This black Lincoln Continental came roaring up and aimed right at her. She's lucky she's young and spry or he'd a had her."

139

"Could you tell what year it was?"

"Yep. I sold cars for almost fifty years and I know cars. It was a year old and in excellent shape."

"Thank you. Miss Rutherford didn't you report a long time ago about someone in a black car shooting at you?"

"Yes, I did. I can't tell if it's the same car. I was too busy getting out of the way."

"I don't know cars," Alice interjected, "but I saw a 967C something and a diamond-shaped decal on the trunk."

"Wonderful. That's more help that I usually get from witnesses. Thank you both for being so observant. Miss Rutherford, do you need me to take you to the hospital?"

"No, thank you. I was going to the real estate office, but I think I'll go home now, take a hot shower and treat my wounds," she laughed. "I'm too old to be jumping and falling around." She thanked Alice and Mr. Hudson for their caring and help. She then limped to her car, got in, clicked her seat belt, looked carefully, then pulled out and drove home.

CHAPTER EIGHTEEN

The next morning she was still limping and her knee hurt as did her elbow. She also had a headache that wouldn't quit. Sleep had been by spurts through the night. She racked her brain trying to think of why she had been targeted. She thought it was best if she didn't drive and called Victoria to see if she could come by and pick her up.

When Victoria and Herb heard about the almost hit and run they were furious.

"I hope they catch the-- " He stopped. "I can't swear in front of you ladies, but I'm plenty mad. I hope the police really follow this up."

"They will," Hannah assured him. "Too much of this has happened. It's obvious someone is after me for some unknown reason. Let's just all be on the alert and stay as safe as possible."

Herb and Victoria started toward their stations. Hannah turned. "Herb, I've been meaning to tell you. I'm so proud of you. How much weight have you lost and you look so fit."

"I now weigh a healthy one hundred ninety and I work out in the gym as often as I can to keep in shape. I feel good about myself now."

Victoria limped up to hug him. "I'm proud of you, too. We've been together so long now that you feel like a brother to me and Hannah is my sister."

"I'm thrilled that we're close and feel so good about each other," Hannah stated, "I hope the new people will fit in as well. Now I need to get busy and call Jim Bridges and Richard Longbow."

They each went to their own work area. Hannah called Jim first and was pleased that he agreed to come for a visit and talk about making the move. It would be another week before he could make the trip, but he'd keep in touch. Richard hesitated and finally said he'd try coming back.

"I've been gone well over a year now and I do look different. Too, I was using an assumed name when I was undercover. I doubt anyone who did this to me will remember me. I'd love to come work with you. Give me directions and I'll be there day after tomorrow."

Hannah was overjoyed and jumped up to tell Victoria and Herb.

"That means we'll have to look for another place seriously," Victoria was thrilled. "When can we start?"

"Herb, I want you to have a say in this. Why don't I call Jane at the real estate office and ask her if she'll be kind enough to bring books and information here to our office. We can all select some places and then check them out."

Jane Goodson was happy to accommodate them and said she would bring books and information over that very afternoon. Her son, Ben, came with her to carry the books. She had some suggestions without realizing how much Hannah's office might need to expand.

Herb, Hannah and Victoria spent a long time looking and discussing. Jane finally realized they wanted a much bigger place.

"Will you need something that large?" she asked puzzled.

"Oh, yes," Hannah replied. "I'm preparing to hire two more and Victoria is almost ready to come in with us. I'll need space for at least six offices plus a receptionist area."

"Good grief. I had no idea you were doing so well."

"We've been so blessed that word of mouth has brought us so many clients."

The three finally selected three possible locations and said they would look and consider them.

"I feel I need them all on the first floor to accommodate the people who might not be able to climb the stairs." Hannah explained.

"This building has an elevator," Ben pointed out to them.

"That's good, but what if there is an electrical storm and the power goes off? Or what if some sick person decides to start a fire and people are trapped on the second floor?" Hannah asked thoughtfully.

Jane laughed. "My goodness. We can't live with what ifs. Life is too short to expect the worst which might never happen."

"I know, but you don't know what threats we've had to face and what dangers we've had to work with," Herb explained. "I agree. We need to be on one floor."

Jan gave a short, embarrassed laugh. "Okay, when do you want to look at the three you've selected?"

The three looked at each other. "Would tomorrow morning be satisfactory with you?" Hannah asked.

"I'll make the time for you. Shall we say ten o'clock?"

"Good. We'll meet you at your office at ten."

"I'll take my van. It will be easier for all of us since I know where we're going," Jane stated.

They looked at all three buildings, but only one came close to what they wanted.

"There are new buildings going up on the other side of town, but they won't be ready for several weeks." Jane informed them.

"Is it possible to see what has been completed and maybe ask for something to be included?" Hannah asked.

"There's only one way to find out," Ben grinned.

They drove about three miles farther and came upon a huge building complex that was partially completed. Ben asked permission to look through some that had interior walls up. The foreman said they could if they would all wear hard hats and stay with him. Of course they agreed.

"I love this view," Hannah and Victoria exclaimed as one and then laughed.

"It doesn't look as if there's but four or five rooms in this unit. Would it be possible for three more rooms to be included in this corner unit?" Hannah asked hopefully.

"Oh, lady. Are you sure you could afford that?"

"I would want it inspected now to be sure all building codes are being followed," Herb said.

The foreman looked angry and then settled. He took out a notepad and started figuring. He showed them the final total. "But the Armstrong Co., who owns this project, would have to agree first."

They thanked him and left. "Now that I know what you really want, I'll keep an eye out for you," Jane assured them as she took them back to their office.

"Thank you Jane, and Ben. We appreciate your interest."

Back in the office the three excitedly talked about what they could do with an office that size and in that great location.

The next day Victoria was alone because Herb and Hannah were both out on cases. She looked up to see who had come in and knew immediately who it was.

"I bet you're Richard Longbow." she said rising to greet him.

"Now how did you guess that, little lady?" he laughed.

"You're all Hannah has been talking about. We have looked forward to seeing you and hopefully having you join us. I'm Victoria Stallard, receptionist, bookkeeper, jack of all trades and have been attending night classes at college to achieve my goal of becoming a detective."

"That's great. How close are you to your goal?"

"At the end of this semester." She proceeded to tell him about the search for a larger office space and possibly hiring Mrs. Harkins. Richard was suitably impressed with the growth of the business and remembered Mrs. Harkins.

Victoria looked at her watch. "It's lunch time and I'm starved. Would you like to join me for lunch and wait for Hannah to come in?"

"I would love to join you. Shall I drive?"

"No. We can walk a few doors down. The food is simple, but good and the prices are more than reasonable."

"Well, I'll gladly buy you lunch, little lady. Are you sure you can walk?" he asked worriedly looking at her brace.

"Oh, yes. I have no trouble that short distance. The agency will pay for our lunch since you are a guest today."

They walked down to the Tasty Bit Diner and had a delicious lunch. They talked and laughed, each telling of their childhood and education. Richard was astonished that they had sat for two hours. Victoria jumped up declaring she had stayed too long and must get back. They walked into the office to find Herb there.

Victoria introduced the two men. Even though Richard was a good six feet, he looked up at Herb. "Brother, you're in the right business," Richard laughed.

Herb explained that he was on the city force and what had happened to his pregnant wife. He told how Hannah had literally whipped him into shape and stood by him.

The more I hear of her, the more I think I might like working here. Too, I need to notify the Chief and the Sheriff before I do anything. Even though I've been dismissed from the force, they might want to use me for something else."

Victoria gave a cry of alarm. "No, they can't have you."

"I have no choice," he laughed. "I must contact them first and discuss this with them. I'm sure Hannah will understand."

"Hannah will understand what?" Hannah spoke behind them. "Richard!"

She ran to hug him. "I'm so glad to see you."

"Yes," Victoria interrupted, "but tell her what you just now told me."

Richard informed Hannah of his responsibilities.

"I understand. You're right, of course. I just hope and pray they'll let you join with us. I need you badly. I need someone and I'd like it to be you."

"I'll do the best I can to explain to them. Thank you, Hannah. Victoria, I'm sincerely glad I met you. Yes, I hope to be working with you. Right now I'm standing at the corner of Ignorance and Bliss. It will take time to determine my future. See you ladies later."

Victoria was charmed with Richard and laughed at his sense of humor.

Herb came in and Victoria could hardly wait to tell him about meeting Richard.

Just before closing, Richard came sauntering in with a big grin on his face. They all rushed to hear what he had to say, but first he had to meet Herb.

"Well," Victoria spluttered, "how much longer must I wait to hear your news?"

"What news?" he asked, teasing her.

"Grrr!" She rushed toward him.

He pretended to be frightened. "Okay, okay. I'll tell you."

"What did they say?" Hannah could hardly wait.

He grinned. "I think they were glad to get rid of me."

A cheer went up from Hannah, Herb and Victoria.

They closed and went out together for a celebration dinner.

"Richard, where are you staying?"

"I'm checked in to the Dew Drop Inn for an indeterminate amount of time."

"Oh, no," Herb stated. "That's too expensive. Come stay with me until you get settled."

"Or you can stay with me," Hannah offered. "I have a guest room."

"Let us men stay together and I'll bring Richard up-to-date on some of our cases, especially the outstanding ones."

The next day Hannah called the foreman of the construction site and asked him when the building would be completed.

"You are giving me a bonus to finish your area, even though the boss doesn't know about it. He would tear my hide off me for concentrating on one."

"I'm truly sorry. But we do need the space like yesterday."

"Ma'am, I'm doing my best. If the weather holds up we should be ready for you in a week."

"Whoopee! I'll love you forever. That will put us in around the third of January."

"Yep. If all goes well. Gotta get back to work."

He hung up before she could express her thanks.

She hurried to tell the others. Richard was sitting in Herb's office going through files. They were all thrilled.

"Can we select the paint and carpeting?" Victoria questioned.

"I don't see why not. I like what we have here." They all agreed with her.

"Okay. I'll drive over tomorrow and inform the foreman what we want. Richard wouldn't you like to ride with me and get an idea of what I have in mind?"

"Nothing would give me greater pleasure, my lady," he gave a courtly bow.

The foreman accepted her ideas, as well he should since she was paying for them. Richard was impressed with the location, the view and the size of their offices. They could see the Atlantic Ocean and were facing elite houses that were far too expensive.

Hannah went by two grocery stores and collected big and medium boxes.

"As we pack, take a magic marker and write on it whose office it is and what the contents are. That way we won't have to be hunting."

As Christmas drew near Victoria wanted to decorate the offices, but agreed to just decorate the front windows.

"There's enough to take down without Christmas decorations," Herb reasoned. "How soon can we select our office?"

"The day before we move in," Hannah assured him. "I have to buy furniture for Richard and others. I'll really be busy."

"Hannah, did you ask Mrs. Harkins to come in with us? Two more weeks and I'll be ready for my own office." Victoria bragged.

"You have to get your license first. I carry liability insurance on all of us. That reminds me, I'll need to talk to my insurance agent about the new offices and there'll be loads more furniture."

Mrs. Harkins had already retired, so Hannah visited her at home.

"Hannah, how delightful. Would you believe I'm getting bored?" Mrs. H. laughed.

"Knowing you and how industrious you are, I can believe it. There is just so much housework for one person. Too, you're accustomed to seeing dozens of people around you and now it's very quiet."

"At first I loved that. Quiet. Now I find that I'm talking to myself. I even took up sewing quilts again," she laughed.

Hannah talked for a few minutes and drank the delicious peppermint tea.

"I really came to offer you a job."

"A job! I just left a good job."

"Mrs. Harkins, I need you badly. I'm moving my offices to a larger area and will have more staff. Victoria has completed her training and is ready to begin work as a detective. By the way, she has her braces off now and is shouting jubilee."

"Oh, the dear girl. I am happy for her. She has suffered so much so far away from family and so young."

"I'm happy to say we're like family in my office," Hannah said. "We really care about each other and are there for each other at any time. You'll love the new men coming in with me, at least one is and I'll know about the second one this week."

"What is it you need me to do?"

"Just what you've been doing, but with less stress and pressure. I need a person to answer the phone, take messages, meet people and help keep my appointments straight. I'll have a bookkeeper, so you won't have any demanding work to do."

"Let me think about it, Hannah. I can't think of anyone I'd rather work with than you. I've looked forward to my retirement, but now I'm getting bored. I sing in the church choir and do volunteer work at the church home for abused women and children. I'm not old, by any means, but neither am I a spring chicken. I don't want to stretch myself so much that I don't enjoy any of it."

Hannah thanked her, gave her a big hug and hurried back to the office. She had two cases she wanted to wind up before the week was out.

Hannah walked into the office and was shocked.

CHAPTER NINETEEN

She was picked up and swung around. "Jim Bridges! You Neanderthal. What do you think you're doing? Put me down."

Laughing with everyone else in the office, he gently stood her beside him.

"I'm so glad to see you. Please tell me that you're going to stay and be part of our staff."

"I'm seriously considering it. I'd have to pass the state bar and be licensed to work in this state. My record is clean though and I don't think I'd have any trouble."

"No. I know you'd have no trouble. I guess you've met everyone."

"Yes, and have even been taken out to see the new location. I approve even though it doesn't mean anything. What would you actually expect of me? I'm not a detective; just a simple lil ole lawyer."

"You're not a simple anything. As far as your duties, we commonly have a question about legal status and clients need an attorney's help more often than you would realize."

Victoria walked toward Hannah. "First Mrs. Harkins was in and is seriously considering your offer. Next," she held up today's newspaper, "there's a big article about another murder and stolen body parts. The mayor is getting angry because nothing has been done to apprehend the criminals. She declares it will ruin our tourist trade."

Herb could hardly contain himself. "Thomas Chandler's trial starts on January 2nd. I hope they jack up the jail and throw him under it, then let it fall heavily." Richard laughed. "Don't laugh. Wait until I tell you what this was about."

Herb took Richard and Jim into his office and told them all about Brian and his babies. He also told them about the murders and the stolen body parts. The two men were upset and angry to hear about all of it.

Jim crossed his legs. "Are you telling me those poor babies, without a mother, have been deprived of their father all this time?

Herb nodded. "And I'm afraid to bring them back yet. There's no telling who Chandler may have hired to do dirt. They're not safe here. As far as we know he doesn't know where they are."

Richard and Jim both made the decision to wait until after the new year to apply for their respective license. Two days until Christmas and Hannah needed a lot of help in packing and notifying everyone of her new address.

Fortunately she would be allowed to keep the same telephone number.

Andrew Rutherford had invited everyone to his house for dinner. He had hired a known and respected caterer to supply the dinner with his suggestions as to what he wanted to serve. It was Christmas Eve and he had the house decorated like a fairy land.

As they drove through the big iron gates they saw a beautifully landscaped lawn. On the right side was a huge creche scene. There were life-sized animals and people. True to those ancient days, the manager was a trough built on the side of the stable, filled with hay. In it lay a doll wrapped in cloths just as Jesus might have been. The statue of Mary, dressed in blue and white, was seated on a bale of hay. Joseph, dressed in brown and carrying a staff, was standing looking down into the manger. Six life-sized angels were hanging across and over the top and a star about thirty-six inches in diameter was over all of this.

"My word," Hannah exclaimed. "Daddy went all out this year. He must think he's Daddy Warbucks. I shudder to think of what we'll find indoors. Look at all those tress decorated at the front. Sheesh."

They all laughed at her attitude. Herb, Victoria, Richard, Jim and Hannah crawled out of the van and hurried indoors. It was cooler than usual for South Carolina and the wind was not friendly.

Andrew met them at the door with a big kiss and hug for his daughter, a hug for Victoria and a back-slipping hand shake for the men. "Welcome. I'm so glad you're here. Knowing you I was afraid you would get tied up with a case and forget about me."

"Now, Daddy, you know I won't do that."

"You've done it before. Introduce me to your friends."

"I'm sorry." She introduced him to Richard and Jim and told that they were planning on being part of the staff.

The mayor, Alice Barker, with her husband, Raymond, was already there. She tottered over in a too tight dress and five inch heels to make her five feet two seem more imposing. "Hello, Hannah. What's this about enlarging your staff? Where will you put everyone?"

"That's part of my big surprise that will be announced in our new opening. I plan to have more detectives, an attorney, a bookkeeper and a receptionist. God has blessed us and we're growing by leaps and bounds."

"It's too bad you can't help catch the butchers leaving bodies all over the place. Maybe we need a new police chief," she quickly walked to the door with a big smile when Chief Wingate and his wife walked in. She air kissed the chief and gave a brief hug to Emily Wingate. "How nice to see you and celebrate the Christmas season together," she gushed.

Everyone looked at each other and rolled their eyes trying not to snicker.

Andrew's three partners and their wives came next and behind them was the city attorney, Lucas Reader, and his wife.

Twenty-one people sat at Andrew's table. He asked a blessing and the people, who were serving, brought in a huge turkey stuffed with sausage, nuts, celery and all good things. There was also dressing and the familiar vegetables including buttered sweet potatoes with marshmallows melted and browned on top. There were also gourmet vegetables and a choice of four desserts. Everyone was stuffed and feeling very good.

With her husband telling her this wasn't the place to discuss it, the mayor stubbornly brought up the subject of the murders and stolen body parts.

Although Andrew did not serve alcoholic beverages, it was obvious that Mayor Barker had plenty. She kept taking something from her purse, which everyone surmised was probably a flask.

"I think I'll fire the police chief and clear the garbage out. Then maybe we'll get some results."

Raymond thanked Andrew for a delicious dinner and told everyone how much he had enjoyed such delightful company. "My wife hasn't been well and I need to get her home for an early night. Thank you again and a very merry Christmas to all. Good night." He hurried her out with her protesting all the way that she hadn't said what she wanted to.

People politely ignored what had happened and discussed the unusually cool weather, world news and what each was hoping for the new year. They all wanted Hannah to tell more of her plans, but she just smiled and changed the subject.

The evening was enjoyable and everyone left before midnight to get to a midnight service at their respective churches. Hannah's church had everyone hold a lit candle in the dark as they sang sweet, old Christmas Carols. At midnight everyone wished each other a merry Christmas, the pastor closed with prayer, and all went home.

Hannah stayed quietly at home on Christmas and assumed all her staff was doing the same. She rested and contemplated her plans for the new office.

Jim and Richard had decided to apply for their license as soon as possible and be ready to move into the new office. Jim's work would require more time as he had to attend classes for South Carolina laws before he could take the bar exam.

The more Mrs. Harkins talked to them the more ecstatic she became. Victoria's classmate, Elizabeth Richardson, had been checked by Chief Wingate and passed with flying colors. Hannah had contacted her about a job as bookkeeper and she was thrilled. She could work and take evening classes if she so desired.

Hannah had suggested a day school near the new office and Elizabeth had quickly checked into it and found it to be just what she wanted. She could leave her little boy each morning on her way to work and Hannah felt it was all right for her to pick him up at three. At that time, if her work was caught up, she could call it a day or bring the boy back to the office with her for a short time. The child was delighted to be playing with other children and then be able to meet real detectives.

The Chief and the Sheriff warned everyone that the noises on New Year's Eve would be possible to cover up crimes. They asked everyone to be on the alert and keep an eye and ear open for trouble. Thankfully there was no damage to Hannah's office.

On January 2nd, Hannah placed a sign on her door giving her new address and the same phone number. A huge truck pulled up to load the furniture in the old office and take it to the new. Victoria had gone over the building and took down all the framed certificates, signs and the plaque. Herb had checked to be sure nothing was left behind, including the water holders.

Richard and Jim came to help set up the new office. Mrs. Harkins had gotten there before any of them and was busily bossing workers as to where the furniture for the front was to be placed.

Another big van pulled up with some new furniture for the additional offices. Elizabeth had left her child with her mother for the day and joined them to set up her office.

The receptionist's office was the same with burbling water and a public restroom. The first room on the left was Elizabeth's with a desk, computer, filing cabinets, the complicated phone and her own person touches.

The first door on the right was to be a conference room. The next one on the right was Hannah's. Across from her was Herb and next to him was Victoria. Jim and Richard had flipped a coin to see who would get which office. Richard won the toss to be next to Hannah and Jim was on his right.

At the end of the hall was a break room with refrigerator, stove, microwave, sink, cabinets, a long couch, two lounge chairs, a table and four chairs and a long mirror on the wall. To the left of the break room was a smaller room as a restroom for ladies and to the right was a smaller room for the gentlemen.

Everyone was pleased with their space and began to put personal touches to their own office. Everyone had their own computer.

Mrs. Harkins had already learned how to answer the very complicated phone and touch the correct button to direct the call. There was a special button on the phone that if it was pushed a siren would sound and bring help.

"Yikes!" Victoria yelped. "I'm going to have to take a class to know how to operate this fool phone."

Richard just shook his head, and said solemnly, "The first time I tried using such a phone, without instruction, I failed abysmally."

"Holy cow," Victoria smacked her forehead, "now the man's a walking dictionary. Hannah, do we have to live with this?"

Laughing everyone went about their business. Elizabeth had taken the books that Hannah provided and proceeded to set up her bookkeeping system. She checked with Victoria's previous records. Mrs. Harkins was busy assimilating knowledge of the material in the files.

Hannah was pleased to discover that the moving men had brought the terra cotta pots with the trees from her front door. They were now in front of the new office.

For a couple of days they were left alone to get settled and get acquainted with the neighborhood. On the third day clients found them and new ones began to trickle in. They were as busy as ever. Jim was almost ready to take his bar exam for S.C. Richard had his local license and was ready to work.

January flew by with all of them too busy to notice how quickly the days went by. February came with slightly warmer weather and flowers peeping out of the ground.

Jim finally took his exam and passed with flying colors. Hannah was jubilant that now she could advertise they had an attorney as well as detectives.

During the third week of February, late one afternoon, Jim and Richard decided to take a stroll along the waterfront to discuss some business and get fresh air. Closing time they staggered in.

Richard had a black eye and a bloody nose. Jim had a cut bottom lip and a long cut on his left cheek. Their clothes looked as if they'd been rolling in the dirt. Richard's shirt was torn and Jim had a hole in the right knee of his pants.

Mrs. Harkins hurried toward them with her hands held out as if to hold back something frightening. "Heavens to Betsy. What happened to you two? Were you mugged?"

"Worse than that," Richard tried to chuckle. "You should see the other guy."

By now Herb, Hannah, Victoria and Elizabeth had joined them giving exclamations of sympathy and anger.

Herb was angry. He forgot himself and started swearing. "WHO DID THIS?"

"Calm down," Jim said, "and we'll tell you."

By now Mrs. Harkins and Elizabeth had wet clean cloths and gently wiped their faces and hands. They were seated on the couch in the break room. "Keep an ear open for someone coming in," Hannah stated just as the front door burst open and Chief Wingate rushed in.

"Where are those imbeciles? They got away before I could talk to them."

Hannah called for him to come back to the break room where he was followed by Lt. James McCormack.

"Well, we've got them under lock and key," the lieutenant told them, "but I want to know how everything came about. What were you doing there and why did you get suspicious of them?"

"Excuse me," Chief Wingate said facetiously. "I could have sworn I'm in command here."

"Oh, I'm sorry. I got carried away. I'm relieved to have the culprits at last and concerned that private citizens put themselves in danger to apprehend them."

"We're all concerned and proud of them," Hannah put in. "I, too, would like to know what happened."

CHAPTER TWENTY

Richard and Jim looked at each other. "Go ahead and tell them," Jim said. "My lip is hurting."

"You're going to need a couple of stitches in that. As soon as you give me a statement, I want you both taken to the hospital for a check up." The chief stated. He took out a tape recorder. "Do you mind if I record this? I want to be sure everything is on the up and up."

He clicked on the recording. "This is February 21, 2013. We're in the office of the Lost Cause Detective Agency, owned by Hannah Rutherford. Present are Lt. James McCormack of the Myrtle Beach, South Carolina city Police, Hannah Rutherford, Mrs. Anna Mae Harkins, Elizabeth Richardson, Detective Victoria Stallard, Detective, Herbert Muller, Detective Richard Longbow, Attorney James Bridges and myself, Chief Ed Wingate of the Myrtle Beach city police force. Detective Richard Longbow and Attorney James Bridges were instrumental in apprehending two persons suspected of committing murder and illegally selling body parts. Detective Longbow, would you like to make a statement?"

"Yes, of course." He cleared his throat. "To begin, I had a problem I wanted to discuss with Jim. We decided to take a walk to talk and pray about it. We each said a short prayer and were talking when we saw ahead of us what looked like some people fighting. We heard a woman's voice yelling to get away and then she screamed. We saw the larger person raise his hand with what looked like something shiny in it.

He looked as if he were going to stab it into the woman. The smaller person was trying to hold the woman and help. We both yelled and took off running toward them. The woman dropped, or was dropped, on the walk and the two people turned to run. We took off after them. I was on the left so I tackled the person on the left and Jim tackled the person on the right. Both of them fought us, but by then others had noticed the altercation and had called for police. They came and placed the two people in handcuffs. We all went back to see about the woman. She was all right but bruised and frightened.

She kept saying, "They were trying to kill me. They had knives.' We discovered that very sharp scalpels had been dropped during the fight. When the police checked, they found igloos with ice in them near where the woman had been standing. They were arrested and taken to jail. We can only assume they are the ones who have been killing innocent people. The smaller person, dressed like a woman, is actually a man. They are what they called partners. The larger person is an intern and the other one just dressed as a nurse to help him and threw everyone off track."

"Just as I thought," Hannah interrupted, "an intern has a lot of college debts and he was probably using this means to pay off his debts."

"Thank God you caught them," Victoria breathed a sigh of relief. "Can you imagine what kind of doctor he would have made?"

Everyone was sitting and thinking when Lt. McCormack spoke. "What you guys did was admirable. Not many people would have jumped in when there were weapons involved.

In fact, some might have yelled a them, but I doubt if many would have tried to apprehend them."

Jim tried to smile through swelling and painful mouth. "Who thought of weapons? I just saw two people jumping on one and felt the odds were uneven. I don't like bullies. Neither do I like to think I might be a coward." He stopped and placed a wet cloth to his mouth while looking miserable.

"I'm escorting you two to the hospital," Chief Wingate declared standing.

"I'll go with them," Hannah stated.

"No," Herb butted in, "you stay here. I'll go with them. It will be less embarrassing to take off their clothes in front of me than in front of you,"

"Why will they need to take off their clothes?" Elizabeth asked. "It's their faces that are injured."

"They'll need to be checked all over for bruises and possible cracked bones."

"Oh," she said meekly.

"Well," Mrs. Harkins jumped up, "now I'm not afraid to walk home alone. We all need to get some rest and be prepared for a full, busy day tomorrow. The press will be over us like ants and media of all kind will be around. There'll also be a lot of nosey people just wanting to be near the so called action." She laughed. "I'm off. Good night everyone. Take good care of our boys." She shook her finger at the Chief. He laughed, put on his hat and followed out after the lieutenant.

Hannah got ready for bed saying a prayer of thanks for the care of Jim and Richard. She smiled thinking that the mayor would be preening in front of all cameras as if she had done the good deed. It would be something to hear her comments.

Two days later Jim and Richard were back at work with stitches, injections and Richard with a cracked rib. They were just grinning at leaving by the back door and avoiding the media. Newspapers and television news continued with the news telling how men who worked at the Lost Cause Detective Agency were the heroes of the hour. Hannah was sorry her friends had gotten hurt, but was thrilled at the great publicity her office was getting.

She was trying to work on a case file when Mrs. Harkins buzzed her phone. "Hannah, I think you'll want to take this call." She had done an admirable job of screening calls.

Hannah pushed the correct button, "Hello, this is Hannah Rutherford."

"Helllooo Miss Rutherford. I owe you so much and I hope someday to do you a favor. You have been a blessing to me."

"Wait a minute. Who is this, please?"

"Hey. I'm sorry. I'm just so happy I'm forgetting myself. This is Alexander Falls. Remember you sent me to another agency to determine if my wife was trying to have me killed?"

"Oh, yes. How are you? What happened?"

"Tracers were placed on the phone, surveillance was carried out, pictures were taken, they were observed meeting and now all are arrested. I don't know exactly what they'll be charged with, but they'll have to face the consequences of their deeds." He chuckled. "I'm so relieved and thank you over and over."

"I'm just happy it turned out well for you. Thank you for telling me."

She hung up smiling. *That's what this work is all about.*

The next week Herb was jumping up in the air and yelling. "Chandler has been sentenced to life in prison without parole. Brian will be too happy to express himself. Hannah, I'm going to offer to drive to Virginia with him and pick up his babies. He wants to go get them himself. Even though he'll have Mrs. Morton taking care of them, he'll need some relief. I want to go any way."

"Be my guest," she laughed. "Do you have any cases pending?"

"Only one and it's fact finding. I can take the time, if it's all right with you."

"Go ahead. Have you ever been to Virginia?"

"No," he said sheepishly. "That's one reason I'd like to go."

"Take long johns. It gets awfully cold up that way. Bring me some Virginia apples. Stop in North Carolina on the way back and get some good clover honey with the comb in it."

"You don't want much, do you?" he teased her.

"Go. Go meet Brian and make your plans. I know he's more excited than you are."

Hannah was settling down to work when Victoria came in looking as if she had lost her last friend. Hannah didn't say anything. She didn't know what to say not knowing what was on Victoria's mind.

Victoria sat down with a big sigh and tears in her eyes. "I've been for an appointment with my doctor." She sobbed. Hannah got up and came around the desk to hug her.

"Would you like to tell me what he said, what is so upsetting to you?"

She kept crying until finally she said through sobs. "He said I've inherited my mother's genetic defect in my heart. I'll need a heart transplant within a year or I'll di di die". She sobbed.

"How fortunate you live in these days with all the advances in medicine. Heart transplants are becoming common now. Your mother didn't have that opportunity."

"I know. I know I'll be in good hands, but I've just earned my license and now I have to give it up." She cried harder.

"No, you won't have to give it up. You'll take a leave of absence and then return stronger than ever."

Herb came in and had to be told. He hugged her. "Little sister, we'll all be beside you fighting with you and God is always with you."

"Little sister?" she almost giggled.

"Yes, you've become very dear to me. All of you have."

Jim came in and was told the news. He was distressed even though he had not known her long. Victoria was an easy person to know and feel affection for since she was such a caring, sweet person.

It wasn't long until all the others came in. Richard suggested that they form a circle and have prayer.

Hannah, Victoria, Herb, Mrs. Harkins, Elizabeth, Jim and Richard stood with arms around each other's shoulders and Richard led in prayer for Victoria to have peace and comfort and for the skill of the doctors. He ended by thanking God for being with Victoria and helping her through this.

The days passed rapidly with Victoria making plans for her surgery as soon as a compatible heart was found.

The last day of February was Victoria's twenty-sixth birthday. Hannah had arranged a surprise party for her and had her family flown in from Minnesota to surprise Victoria. Even the nieces and nephews were to be included. She had told the family of Victoria's health problems and they had promised to make it a celebration for her. Victoria's mother was fifty-one when she died with a heart defect, but everyone was hopeful that Victoria would get excellent medical care.

At six Hannah told everyone to get ready and she was going to take everyone to the Seacoast Grill for a birthday dinner for Victoria. Needless to say, Victoria was surprised and very pleased.

They drove down and parked in a valet area. They went in together in such a way that Victoria and Hannah came in last. Victoria walked innocently and calmly behind the group until they got to the reserved seating area. Everyone stood aside so Victoria could see who was seated at the tables. She gave a cry of joy, hugging her father and the whole family.

Everyone took turn about helping her wipe the tears from her eyes.

"Gee sis, I didn't know we'd make you so miserable or we wouldn't have come," he teased her.

"Shush," she slapped his chest. "Brother dear, I love you, but you're not funny. Everyone knows these are tears of joy."

The lobster and shrimp almost went unnoticed with everyone trying to talk and bring Victoria up-to-date on family business. After the dinner, she hugged Hannah and thanked her and then hugged all her co-workers. She elected to go to the hotel rooms and continue visiting with her family as they were flying home again the next day.

The next day Victoria was bubbling with joy and appreciation for her birthday and for Hannah bringing her family together. "You think I'm dying, don't you, and you wanted us to have one last time together."

"No, silly. Get that out of your head this minute. It was just a love gift for all you've meant to me. I knew how long it had been since you saw your entire family. The children are precious and the two new babies made me wish I had made different plans."

Victoria looked surprised. "You mean you wanted a husband and children? Why didn't you ever get serious about all those fellows that kept fluttering around you?"

"I wasn't ready because I was concentrating on developing this business. Don't count me out yet. I'm not too old."

"I know you aren't, and you'll make a wonderful wife and mother."

Richard came in to hear the last statement. He asked surprised, "Hannah, are you getting married? I didn't even know you were seeing anyone."

"I'm not. I'm not." She assured him. "We're just talking."

"Whew. That's a relief."

"What do you mean?" Victoria asked with 'ruffled feathers'. "What does it matter to you what she does?"

Richard looked like a little boy that had been caught in something he shouldn't. "Maybe it's because I'm interested and hoped I'd stand a chance with her."

Hannah was too surprised to speak, but not Victoria. "Well, dummy. All you have to do is ask."

Richard looked embarrassed. "Hannah, would you consider going to the Civic Center dance with me Saturday? We could have supper somewhere before we go or eat later in the evening."

"Well, whoop-ti-do. How romantic can you get? Did you expect her to fall at your feet with that invitation?"

"Victoria!" Hannah finally found her voice. "Stop teasing Richard." She looked at him. "I hadn't thought about going, but I'd love to go with you and whatever plans you make will be fine."

With a shy smile and a sigh of relief he ducked his head and walked back to his office.

Hannah let Victoria knew she was disappointed in her behavior. "You're like my big sister and I love you. I want the best for you." Victoria explained.

"What makes you think Richard isn't the best?"

"Not one blessed thing. I guess he just surprised me."

"He surprised me, too, but now I'm glad he asked. Now let's all get to work."

Hannah walked out and told Mrs. Harkins that she was going to see Attorney Archibald Worthington about her will. "After hearing about Victoria's problems, I thought I should bring my will to current status."

"There's nothing wrong with you, is there, Hannah?" Mrs. Harkins asked worriedly.

"Oh, no. I'm just doing what all of us should do and keep everything current." She left and was gone almost two hours.

When she returned the group was waiting anxiously for her return.

"For pity's sake," she was exasperated, "what do all of you think you're doing?"

"We love you and are worried that there is something you're not telling us."

"What ever gave you that foolish idea?"

"You wanted to check your will. We were afraid there might be something wrong that we didn't know about." Elizabeth spoke softly.

"And after my glorious news, we're all concerned about each other." Victoria declared.

"How many times do I need to reassure you? There's. Nothing. Wrong."

"Okay. Okay. We're sorry," Herb rushed to say. "We just care."

"I know and I love you all, but I'm going to be around for such a long time, you're going to be sick of me."

Little did she know that this was an untrue statement.

CHAPTER TWENTY-ONE

A week later, Hannah started out of the office an hour early.

"Where are you headed?" Mrs. Harkins called after her.

"To my house where I shall be perfectly safe. Is that all right with everyone?"

They all laughed with her. Victoria called, "May I go with you? I need to discuss something very personal with you."

"Oh course. Come on."

Hannah pulled her car into the garage and Victoria pulled up behind her in the driveway. Hannah waited on her so she could push the button to pull the door down. They walked into the kitchen.

Hannah stopped. "Something is not right."

"What is it?" Victoria asked worriedly.

"I don't know, but the feeling in the house isn't right."

At that two men stepped out of the hall and stood in the door of the kitchen. They were dressed all in black with black ski masks and black gloves. Even their shoes were black sneakers. They each had a device on their necks which caused their voices to sound garbled.

"You're smart police lady, and you've outwitted us many times, but your clock has run down."

"Get out of here or we'll call the police. If you leave now they won't be able to find you." Victoria tried to reason with them. They just laughed loud and long.

One pointed a pistol and shot just as Hannah tried to run at them. He jerked and shot her in the leg. The blood spurted as Victoria kept screaming loudly enough to alert the entire neighborhood. In fact, men were out in their lawns trying to determine where the screaming was coming from.

"Idiot," the second man yelled, "now you've done it." He too pointed a dart gun at her and yelled, "Get out of here. I've shot her with a dose. The poison will get her." They both ran out the back door, jumped over the hedge between the next house and ran down the back alley.

Two neighbor men finally located where the trouble was and ran in. They could not stop Victoria from screaming. By now several neighbors had gathered.

One neighbor ran to the kitchen wall phone and called 9-1-1. By then some women had taken Victoria in hand and quietened her enough to ask her whom they should call. She finally gave them the office phone.

The ambulance was just leaving when Herb, Jim and Richard drove up. They found Hannah was being taken to the Seacoast Medical Center. They took Victoria with them and quickly drove there.

They were not allowed in where she had been taken. Victoria finally got herself together enough to call Hannah's father, Andrew. He was shocked and devastated. Common sense told him he shouldn't drive, so he asked a friend to drive him.

Hannah's staff was elated to see him because now they could get some news. Her father was the only one allowed back in the surgery unit. He came back about ten minutes later followed by a Doctor Huw Chang. The doctor said Mr.

Rutherford had given permission for him to tell them what had happened to Hannah.

He patiently explained. "First Miss Rutherford has lost a tremendous amount of blood and her blood pressure is dropping dangerously low. We are giving her transfusion constantly."

"But she'll be all right, won't she?" Several spoke at once.

"That I can't say. We're working better than the best of our ability to save her."

"When will we know for sure?" Richard asked.

"I don't know that either. I'm sorry, but I need to get back to help the team that is working with her."

"Wait," Herb spoke quickly. "You haven't told us what the damage is."

Dr. Chang looked at Andrew and he nodded his head. His eyes were red from crying and he looked ages older in his grief.

"The bullet fortunately missed the kneecap. It did go through to tear the femoral artery back of the knee which has caused the alarming blood loss. The unusually large transfusion has diluted some of the important factors in the blood and prevents the blood from coagulating. Internal organs, like the kidneys, can collapse. The next few hours are critical. We'll take a vein from her other leg to repair the torn artery. Now I really must go."

By now Mrs. Harkins and Elizabeth had joined them. The staff was around Andrew for prayer.

In about six hours, Dr. Chang and a Doctor Grant Morton came to them.

Dr. Chang looked beaten. "I'm sorry. We did all we could, but we could not save her."

The staff, men and women, were holding each other and crying. Andrew collapsed and was taken into ICU to be sure his heart did not fail him. He did hear Dr. Morton speak to Victoria.

"Miss Stallard, if you're prepared, Miss Rutherford's heart is compatible for you. We can do the transplant this morning if ------"

"No." she cried. "I can't take Hannah's heart."

With tears streaming down his cheeks, Richard placed an arm around Victoria's shoulder. "Honey, Hannah would want you to have it. You know she would. She loved you very much and would want this for you."

"I'll have to think about it."

"There isn't time to think. It has to be done within the next hour." Dr. Morton informed her.

The staff kept urging her. "You're an adult and can sign your own papers," James told her. "We'll notify your family. Please, please do this."

A nurse came out and told her Mr. Rutherford wanted to speak to her.

"Victoria, I heard the offer of Hannah's heart. She would want you to do this. Please take it and I'll always feel that part of my baby is still with me."

Victoria reluctantly and fearfully gave in. There was no formal funeral for Hannah as everyone was involved in something heartbreaking. A month later, Victoria was up and felt wonderfully well, but still not ready for a full day's work.

A week later Archibald Worthington called the staff in for the reading of Hannah's will. She did not include her father except to give him all her love, because he was wealthy in his own right. She had decided that Victoria and Herb would be co-owners of the business and everyone was to get a substantial monetary bonus in addition to her gifts to charities. She did stipulate that everyone was to keep their job if they wanted it.

The staff held a private meeting and voted to make Victoria and Herb Presidents and Jim and Richard Vice Presidents. Mrs. Harkins was to keep her job as long as she wanted it as was Elizabeth

A few days later the newspaper had printed all this information even though no one knew how the news got out. One day a very drunk mayor, Alice Barker, came staggering into the office.

"You low lifes think you're so smart carrying on the precious, Hannah's work. She was no saint. She arrested my twin sister's son and her old man prosecuted him. He was sent to prison for life with no parole. My twin sister was so heartbroken over her son that she committed suicide. See, your precious Hannah was no saint. I thought I'd never get rid of her. My men kept doing a lousy job until one finally got it right." She giggled and staggered around.

"Are you trying to say," Richard said through clinched teeth, "that you had Hannah killed."

"Yeah." She stuck a foul-smelling bleary eyed face right in his. "And none of you idiots caught on. See, I'm the smartest."

Victoria had called and the newly created Sgt. Liam O'Brien had eased into the office. He placed handcuffs on Alice and over her loud protests took her off to jail.

"Whew. It's a good thing he took her out of here before I got into trouble by strangling her," Richard declared. They all agreed.

Victoria was very proud of Liam because he was seeing her seriously now.

Richard ran in the office a few days later. "You folks remember when Hannah came to Florida to find information about a bigamous husband and an innocent second wife?"

Yes, they remembered even though they weren't familiar with the case. Richard was eager to share the news and James was eager to hear since he had also been involved.

"That upstanding military officer has been court martialed, stripped of all rank and jailed, and all his holdings have been given to his legal first wife. She was sweet enough to allow Anna Marie to keep her house and the local bank account. All's well that ends well," he finished with a big grin.

A beautiful memorial service was held for Hannah. It seemed the entire town was present. Andrew sat with bowed head and the comfort of Hannah's staff around him. Dozens of people stood and told how Hannah had come to their aid, sometimes with actions and sometimes with money.

The Myrtle Beach Police Pipe Band played "Flowers of the Forest" which was a tribute to fallen soldiers. They then played "Scotland the Brave" and ended with "Amazing Grace". A bugler played taps with loud sobs filling the sanctuary.

Two days later Herb called a staff meeting to discuss how the business was to be carried on. "Our former mayor is in the insane hospital."

"Now I think we'd all get busy and make this office grow as Hannah would have. Victoria, I'm so happy that you're able to work and are doing so well. I understand that wedding bells may be ringing for you and Liam soon," Herb said.

"Yes, and I'm happy, too," she said flashing a sparkling diamond. "I know I'm going to do a bang up good job because I have a true detective's heart."

Sioux Dallas playing her bagpipes at an army base in Washington, D.C. She was a marching member of the Gulf Coast Pipes and Drums.

Dear Readers,

I promised to tell you about a few of the first women detectives before I share the recipes with you.

ISABELLA MARIE BOYD (Belle Boyd) was born on May 9, 1844 in Martinsburg, Virginia (now West Virginia) the oldest child of Benjamin and Mary Rebecca Glenn Boyd. She was a tomboy climbing trees with her brothers and running races with them. She was highly intelligent and well educated. After preliminary schooling she attended the Mount Washington Female College at the age of twelve and finished at the age of sixteen.

Her career began by chance as a spy and then as a detective. On July 4, 1861, a group of Union soldiers saw the Confederate flag flying outside her home. They tore it down and hung a Union flag in its place. She tried to fight the men and didn't get anywhere until one of the men cursed Belle's mother and called her filthy names. Belle went inside, got a gun and killed him. She was arrested, but released due to the circumstances.

Some of the Union soldiers felt sorry for her and befriended her. She listened to their plans and then gave her house worker, Eliza Hopewell, a message to be carried to Confederate General Stonewall Jackson. Eliza carried the message in a hollowed-out watch case and sometimes in hollowed-out vegetables.

Belle was caught and told she could be put to death. She stood straight and looked them in the eye without showing fear. They let her go. General Jackson made her an aide-de-camp on his staff. She then became a member of the

Confederate Secret Service using assumed names to attend social affairs and find information. Belle entertained Union officers in her home and listened to their plans which she passed along. On July 29, 1862 she was arrested and held for a month in Old Capitol Prison in Washington, D.C. She contacted typhoid fever and on December 1, 1863 was sent to England for treatments.

While in England she married Samuel Hardinge. He was captured in Canada where he died. Belle started a stage career singing and telling war stories. She died on June 11, 1900 while touring the western United States.

She is buried in Spring Grove Cemetery in Kilbourne City, Wisconsin.

PAULINE CUSHMAN was born Harriet Wood in New Orleans. When the war began she was a loyal unionist. The Union used her to attend gatherings and discover who the spies were and to listen to any information they could use.

In May, 1863 General Rosecrans prepared to drive General Bragg across the Tennessee River. She was sent as an actress entertaining the troops to find information on the location and strength of Bragg's military. She was captured and ordered to be hung. Before she could be hung in Shelbyville, Tenn., Gen. Bragg was attacked and left in a hurry forgetting Cushman in jail. She was rescued by Union troops and given the rank of Major which she demanded to be addressed as -- Major Cushman.

She was married three times and neither was a good marriage. After the war she had no luck getting work as an actress. She became a dressmaker's assistant and later cleaned houses for people. She began taking opium and died of an overdose on December 2, 1893. The Grand Army of the Republic insisted on burying her with honors in a military cemetery in San Francisco.

NANCY HART was born in 1846 in Raleigh, North Carolina. Her mother was first cousin to Andrew Johnson who later became President. When Nancy was fourteen, she joined the Moccasin Rangers, riding and shooting as good as any man.

The Union soldiers killed many civilians needlessly. Nancy hated this and at the age of eighteen in July, 1861, led a raid against the Union. She was captured, but tricked her guard and killed him with his own gun. She later married Joshua Douglas. The date of her death is unknown.

KATE WARNE was the first recognized female detective in the United States. She was born in New York City and married at a young age. Her husband died of an illness soon after the wedding.

A childless widow, she was searching for a means of income. Allen Pinkerton of the Pinkerton Detective Agency advertised for detectives. In 1856 she went in to apply for a job. He thought at first that she wanted a secretarial position. He was astonished when he learned she wanted to be a detective. At 10 a m on August 23, 1856 she had convinced him to give her a try.

Kate was very good at assuming other names and occupations so that she could infiltrate a business or a home and gain the information needed. If a man was suspected of embezzlement, or a more serious crime, she would make friends with his wife or members of his family. They would learn to trust her and talk in front of her.

Allen Pinkerton was hired by Samuel H. Felton, President of Wilmington and Baltimore Railroad, to investigate some criminal activities. Kate was one of the five agents sent to Baltimore, Maryland on February 3, 1861 to investigate. Her evidence proved that there were plots against the railroad and plots to assassinate president - elect Abraham Lincoln. The people told Kate that if Lincoln came through Baltimore, he would leave in a casket.

She called herself Mrs. Cherry, a rich, southern lady staying at the Barnum Hotel. She passed herself off as a "flirting" southern bell and was able to gain valuable information.

Lincoln was traveling by train from his home in Springfield, Illinois to Washington, D.C. with stops along the way to campaign. Transfers had to be made. One ended at Calvert Street and another at Camden Street. The distance between the two stations was about a mile and was covered by horse-drawn carriage.

Kate learned that as Mr. Lincoln would enter his carriage, a plan was made for some men to pretend to start a big street fight. It was thought the police would go to stop the fight leaving Mr. Lincoln unprotected. A few other men were supposed to murder him there and then run to get on a steamer in the Chesapeake Bay and escape. Pinkerton asked Kate to take the 5:10 p m train, on February 18, and take a letter to Norman B. Judd informing him of the plot.

On February 21, Judd, Pinkerton and Lincoln met to make plans. A detective was to be disguised as Lincoln and be prepared to fire on the would-be murderers. The plot was confirmed by Frederick W. Seward, son of William H. Seward, secretary of state designated.

Mr. Lincoln was duty bound to give some speeches, raise an American flag at Independence Hall and attend an very important political dinner. John George Nicolay, Lincoln's private secretary, came to get him from the dinner saying it was something vitally important they needed to discuss. Lincoln put on a traveling suit, a soft felt cap and a shawl to look like an invalid.

The disguised Lincoln took the sleeping car. Allen Pinkerton and other detectives were nearby, Kate walked through the train and loudly said goodnight to Mr. Lincoln so those listening would not catch on to the switch. Kate did not sleep the whole time she was on duty which was many hours through night and day. In the meantime the real Mr. Lincoln, with other detectives, was traveling safely on the Pennsylvania Railroad. As the entire idea for protecting Mr. Lincoln was Kate's idea, Pinkerton was quick to tell everyone she was as good as any man on his force.

During the War Between The States, Pinkerton and Kate were hired to gather information. She went undercover as a socialite where a man would not have been believable. She was able to overhear a lot of useful information.

Kate served well and Pinkerton was loud in his praise of her. He began to hire other women who would be trained by Kate Warne, Supervisor of Women Agents.

On January 1, 1868, Kate became very ill with pneumonia and on the 28th died with Pinkerton holding her hand. He had her buried in the Pinkerton Family Cemetery (Graceland Cemetery) in Chicago, Illinois. The stone reads Kate Warne died of congestion of the lungs at the age of 38. She was buried with full honors on January 30, 1868.

Women were not allowed to be on a police force until 1891 and were not listed as detectives until 1903.

SOME TASTY TREATS TO ENJOY FROM SIOUX DALLAS

Don't forget when mixing anything, stir in one item at a time and mix before adding another item. This improves the flavor and the texture of the food. Use regular sugar -- NO SUBSTITUTES.

South Carolina is famous for Chicken Bog. It is as traditional a dish as any other special holiday food. It is easy to prepare and can be cooked for any number of people. Hobos would cook it in black iron pots on the banks of the Pee Dee River. Older people believe it was started years ago at the tobacco barn warehouses. Men would cook it and serve with coleslaw.

Today they have days of celebration and Chicken Bog cook-offs which is as famous as the Texas chili cook-offs. It is a day of arts and crafts booths, sometimes rides for children and dozens of booths where people compete for the best recipe for Chicken Bog.

Mrs. Chisholm Wallace of Red Doe Plantation has been known for her recipe served with coleslaw and cornbread.

There were about thirty recipes which would be too boring to discuss and take too much time and space, I choose Mrs. Wallace's to share with you.

Chicken Bog

About a six pound fat hen
1 small onion
1 small green pepper
1 stick of butter (¼ pound)
2 pounds of long grain white rice (NOT INSTANT RICE)
One fourth lb. lean bacon
Salt and pepper to taste
Six quart heavy aluminum pot with lid

Wash chicken and put it in the pot with enough water so that there will be at least six cups of broth after chicken has cooked. Cook until very tender. When cooked, take from stove and let cool enough to handle it.

Pull the meat from the bones throwing away any fat and skin. Skim fat from broth. Tear meat into bite-sized pieces. Wash the pot and cook the bacon slowly in it until it is crisp, but not burned. Remove bacon. Leave bacon grease in the pot and put in the chopped up onion and pepper. Brown slightly. Add six cups of chicken broth and season to taste. Boil rice in another pot stirring as seldom as possible so as to not make the rice gooey. In the aluminum pot place the stick of butter on low heat. Add all the other ingredients, including the chicken pieces and rice, cooking slowly for about an hour. Crumble bacon and place on top of a serving. Bog can be kept in the refrigerator or frozen and later reheated.

Garbanzo Bean Salad

Thirty ounces of garbanzo beans drained and rinsed (2 cans)
3 Roma tomatoes, sliced
2 spring onions chopped with green tops
5 or 6 radishes sliced
Juice of 3 limes
2 tablespoons of virgin olive oil
One half cup of feta cheese
1 teaspoon kosher salt
One half teaspoon each of garlic powder and black pepper
Lettuce salad mix of your choice
Mix all ingredients tossing gently.
Serve with fancy crackers or bread of choice

Seafood Egg Scramble

2 ounces of fresh crab meat
1 teaspoon olive oil
2 large eggs
1 or 2 ounces shredded cheese
Sauté the crab meat in olive oil on medium heat, Add lightly beaten eggs and stir. Add the cheese and gently stir for a minute. Add salt and pepper to taste. Serve hot with bread of choice.

Martha Washington Pie

Preheat oven on 375 degrees
1 cup softened butter
2 cups white sugar
2 eggs lightly beaten
1 teaspoon vanilla extract
1 tablespoon unsweetened cocoa powder
2 teaspoons baking powder
1 cup milk
2 cups all purpose flour
Three fourths cup golden raisins
1 cup chopped walnuts (I use black walnuts)
2 unbaked pie crusts

<u>Icing</u>
1 cup confectioner sugar
One half teaspoon vanilla extract
4 tablespoons milk

Gently mix butter, sugar, eggs, cocoa powder, baking powder, milk, flour until smooth. Stir in raisins and walnuts. Pour in pie crusts and bake.

For the icing, combine the sugar and vanilla. Gradually stir in the milk until desired consistency is reached. Take baked pies out of the oven and cover with icing. Serve warm.

The next few do not have a title. I don't know where they originated.

(1) Combine one fourth ounce of active dry yeast with one cup warm water and stir. Gradually add 1 teaspoon sugar and let stand about five minutes. Add 1 cup evaporated milk and 2 large slightly beaten eggs. Add a pinch of salt and one fourth cup of sugar and let dough stand to rise.

Shape into small squares about 2 inches. Bake at 375. Take out while still hot and roll in confectioner sugar. Can be served with honey.

(2) For a crunchy low calorie snack:
2 cups spoon-sized shredded wheat (cereal-not frosted)
1 heaping tablespoon peanut butter (I use crunchy)
1 cup of melted light or dark chocolate
Confectioner sugar

Melt peanut butter and chocolate together. Stir in shredded wheat. Lift each one out with a spoon and let dry. Optional to give second "bath". Roll in confectioner sugar. Lick your fingers and enjoy.

(3) Open a can of biscuits. Take one biscuit and break the slices apart. (You might want to use 2 slices together. In the center place your favorite fruit and chopped nuts if desired. Crimp up the edges together and bake according to directions. You now have a bite-sized treat. I cook these while camping out in a Dutch oven. (It sounds as if I camp in the oven.)

(4) Boil a dozen eggs. Peal and place in a glass jar or bowl with a top. Add a can of pickled beets with juice and one full cup of apple cider vinegar. Let stand for at least 2 days. I love my pickled eggs. You might want more vinegar according to taste.

Butter Pecan Icing in the Cake

Preheat oven to 350
Baking dish
Do not follow baking directions on box.
Box of Betty Crocker Butter Pecan cake mix
Can of Betty Crocker Coconut - Pecan frosting
4 eggs
1 cup water
Three-fourths cup chopped pecans
One-half cup vegetable oil

On low speed mix oil, water, eggs and frosting together. Add cake mix and pecans. Mix on low speed until completely combined (about 1 minute).

Pour into baking dish and bake 35 to 40 minutes. Use a toothpick to test if it is done in the middle. Optional to sprinkle with powdered sugar. Serve as is or with ice cream.

Stuffed Mushrooms (This is my recipe.)

Buy large mushrooms. Wash thoroughly. Snap out the stems and either throw away or eat separately. You need a pound of Jimmy Dean's sage sausage. Pinch a piece of sausage and put it in the mushroom caps. Melt butter in a baking dish. Place the mushroom, cap down, in the butter and bake at 300 for about three minutes. Make sure the sausage is done. Stick a toothpick in each one and serve hot as an hors d'oeuvre.

Shrimp Cashew

1 pound cleaned medium shrimp
1 tablespoon plus 1 teaspoon cornstarch
One fourth teaspoon of each: sugar, baking soda, salt
Pinch of pepper
1 cup whole cashews (break apart)
One half cup vegetable oil
Three cups cooked rice
Optional to add celery, peppers, etc.

Gently stir everything together except the rice and shrimps. Let stand about fifteen minutes. Heat over medium heat. Add shrimp. Stir constantly. Place serving over rice. Serve hot.

Corn Pudding

Preheat oven to 400
5 large eggs
One third cup melted butter
One fourth cup sugar
One half cup milk
4 tablespoons cornstarch
30 ounces whole kernel corn
May add a can of cream style corn if desired

Lightly beat eggs. Add melted butter, sugar and milk. Gently stir. Add cornstarch. Stir in corn blending well. Pour into casserole dish and bake for one hour.